Stacey and the Missing Ring

Other books by
Ann M. Martin

Ma and Pa Dracula
Yours Turly, Shirley
Ten Kids, No Pets
Slam Book
Just a Summer Romance
Missing Since Monday
With You and Without You
Me and Katie (the Pest)
Stage Fright
Inside Out
Bummer Summer

BABY-SITTERS LITTLE SISTER series
THE BABY-SITTERS CLUB series
(see back of the book for a complete listing)

Stacey and the Missing Ring

Ann M. Martin

SCHOLASTIC INC.
New York Toronto London Auckland Sydney

Cover art by Hodges Soileau

ISBN 0-590-44084-5

12 11 10 9 8 7 6 5 4 3 2 1 1 2 3 4 5 6/9

Printed in the U.S.A. 28

First Scholastic printing, August 1991

The author gratefully acknowledges
Ellen Miles
for her help in
preparing this manuscript.

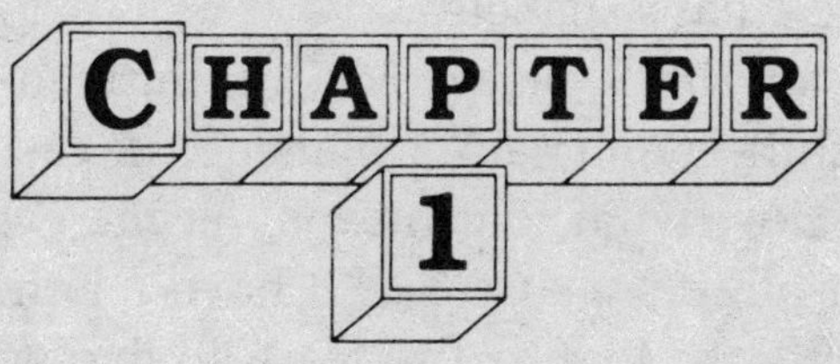

Please don't tell any of my friends. They'd think I was nuts if they knew. But it's true. Sometimes I actually like to clean house.

Maybe you know what I mean. There can be something really satisfying about taking that last swipe with a mop, or polishing a faucet until it shines, or looking at a newly cleaned window with the sun sparkling through it.

Or maybe you just think I'm nuts.

Anyway, whether you agree with me or not, you'll have to take my word for it. I was having a good time that Saturday morning, helping my mother clean the house. Cleaning wasn't all we'd done, though.

First, we'd made breakfast — or rather, my mom made breakfast, and I ate it. She cooked my favorite: blueberry pancakes. I love them because they're naturally sweet, so I don't miss the oceans of maple syrup that most people drown their pancakes in.

I can't have maple syrup on my pancakes because I have diabetes.

That's right. I, Stacey McGill, thirteen-year-old eighth-grader, am a diabetic. In case you don't know what that means, let me explain. First of all, it's a disease I'll have for the rest of my life, so I've had to learn to live with it. My pancreas (that's one of those weird-shaped organs inside you) doesn't do its job right. It doesn't make this stuff called insulin, which people need to help them digest carbohydrates and sugar.

Since my body can't handle sugar too well, I have to be very, very careful about what I eat and when I eat it. Also, I have to supply the insulin that my pancreas can't. How do I do that? Well, I give myself shots every day. I know, ew-ew-ew, right? But it's not so bad once you get used to it.

And I don't have a choice, anyway. If I don't take care of myself, I can get really sick. In fact, not too long ago, I found that out for sure. I slipped a little on my diet and stopped taking care of myself the way I should, and guess what. I landed in the hospital. I don't want that to happen again any time soon, so

I'm back to being Little Miss Healthy of Stoneybrook, Connecticut.

Stoneybrook's the town where my mom and I live. We didn't always live here, though. I grew up in New York City — and boy, did I love New York. I used to be a real New Yorker — I loved shopping at Bloomingdale's, going to the Hard Rock Cafe, seeing musicals on Broadway. But you know what? Now I love Stoneybrook, too.

My family first moved from New York to Stoneybrook a while back, when my dad got transferred by his company. We adjusted pretty well to the move — in fact, I was really, really happy in Stoneybrook. Not too long after we'd moved there, I became a member of this great club — a baby-sitting club. I'd always loved to baby-sit, and joining the club was like getting a whole bunch of best friends all at once.

But the club's another story. I'll tell you more about that later. I'm just trying to explain why I was so happy in Stoneybrook — so that you'll understand what a shock it was when my dad got transferred *back* to the city and we had to leave!

Guess what. Once we were back in New York, my parents started to fight a lot, and before long they'd decided to get a divorce. Then my dad decided to get a little apartment on the East Side of Manhattan, and my mom decided to move back to Stoneybrook, where she'd been happy. It was up to me to choose where I wanted to live.

I hope you never have to make a decision like that.

It wasn't easy, but finally I realized that I would be happiest living with my mom in Stoneybrook. I do visit my dad fairly often, and I love being in New York on those weekends, but you know what? I think I made the right decision. It's tough being a "divorced kid" (I'm still trying to figure it all out), but here in Stoneybrook I have a lot of good friends to help me through it.

Also, I've gotten pretty close to my mom, and I think we make a good team. Like on that Saturday morning. She would dust the furniture, and I would polish it. She would sweep the floor, and I would mop it. We were working well together.

Mom had tuned the radio to an oldies station, and we were having a blast singing along to these songs that had been popular when she was a teenager. Over the years she's taught me the words to a lot of them, so now I can "Do the Twist" and "Shake it up, Baby" with the best of them.

I'd just been dancing with the mop to "I Wanna Hold Your Hand," when the song ended and Roy Orbison came on singing "Pretty Woman." My mom wandered into the kitchen with a faraway look in her eyes. "I love that song," she said. "It always reminds me of my sixteenth birthday."

It's hard to imagine your mother as a sixteen-year-old.

"Did you have a sweet-sixteen party?" I asked.

"Are you kidding? I had the biggest, best sweet-sixteen party of the decade. Didn't I ever show you the pictures?" She dragged me into the living room and sat me on the couch. Then she pulled an old, beat-up photo album off the shelf.

"Oh, right," I said, as soon as I saw the pictures. "Now I remember. That's where you were wearing that funny dress, and you had that weird hairdo — what's it called? A wasps' nest?"

"A beehive," she said, laughing. "And I don't think my dress was so funny. It was my first real grown-up dress, and I had high heels to match. I felt like a million dollars that day."

We looked at the pictures together. "You do look happy," I said.

"I always loved to celebrate my birthday," Mom told me. "And that one was the most fun of all."

"I love my birthday, too." I said. Then I remembered something I'd been meaning to bring up. "In fact," I added in a rush, deciding that now was as good a time as any, "since my birthday has always had such a special meaning for me, I was wondering if you might like to help me buy this ring I saw at the Stoneybrook Jeweler's." There. I'd said it.

"Ring?" asked my mother. "What does this have to do with your birthday? Your birthday is months away." She closed the photo album and looked at me.

"I know," I said. "And I didn't mean that the ring would be a birthday present. See, it's a birthstone ring. It's gorgeous, and it would be so — so *meaningful* for me." I looked at her hopefully. "I just thought that maybe you could help me pay for it."

Actually I had hoped that she would *buy* it for me, but I was already getting the feeling that there was no way *that* was going to happen.

"What is your birthstone, Stacey?" Mom asked. She wasn't making any offers, I noticed.

"Well," I answered. "It's — it's a diamond." Somehow I knew she wasn't going to be thrilled with that news.

"Diamond, hmm?" she said. "I'm not sure a diamond ring is appropriate for a girl your age." She frowned.

"Lots of girls have birthstone rings!" I said. Actually, I only knew two girls who had them, and neither of their birthstones was a diamond. I think one was an amethyst and one was a garnet. I was pretty sure that neither cost quite as much as a diamond. But I kept that to myself.

"Lots of girls . . ." said my mother. "Well. How much does the ring cost?"

Suddenly I wondered if I'd picked the right time for this after all. Mom and I had been having such a nice time together, and now things were about to turn sour. Even so, I gritted my teeth and told her how much the ring cost.

I thought my mom was going to faint.

"Anastasia Elizabeth McGill!" she said. "You *have* to be kidding. Don't you think that's a little *extravagant*?"

"I — I just thought that we might be able to afford — " I started to say.

"Afford a diamond ring?" she interrupted. "It seems to me that there are plenty of better ways for us to spend money."

Uh-oh. This wasn't going in the right direction at all.

"Now, I might be willing to give you ten dollars toward the ring," Mom went on, "but that's it. I certainly can't — and won't — *buy* it for you."

Ten dollars! Ten dollars wouldn't go far toward that ring. I'd have to baby-sit every day for the rest of my life to make up the difference. All of a sudden I got mad. I don't ask my mom for much, and now she was acting as if I were being outrageous.

"Dad would buy it for me," I muttered.

"What?" she asked. "Did you say what I think you said?"

"Dad would buy it for me," I repeated more loudly. So what if she was mad. I was, too.

"You know," she said, kind of sadly, "you may be right about that."

For a moment I felt bad. "I know you don't make as much money as Dad does," I said. "But — "

"There's no but about it, Stacey," she said. "I *don't* make as much as he does, and money is always going to be tighter in Stoneybrook than it is in New York. But you can't have everything you want."

"But I don't ask for everything!" I said. "It's just this one ring."

But my mom wasn't even listening. She was off on another track by then. "You know, Stacey, ever since you got sick, your father and I have been trying hard not to put you in the middle of our arguments," she said.

"I know," I answered. "And I appreciate it." (Sometimes I used to feel like a Ping-Pong ball being batted around, but when I was sick, I had a talk with my parents. They had promised to change.)

"And I've been trying to make sure not to ask you for too much information about your father," Mom continued. She used to pump me all the time about what we did and where we went. I was glad she'd stopped. "But," Mom continued, "I can't help noticing that you come home with all kinds of nice things every time you visit him. He's treating you like a princess when you're in New York, and I don't think it's good for you."

"But he's not, really!" I said. It was true that when the divorce first happened, Dad sometimes bought me incredibly expensive stuff, trying to make up for all the pain he thought he'd put me through. But now he knew that I didn't need — or want — him to do that. He still bought me presents, I'll admit, but small things, mostly.

Actually, I wasn't sure Dad *would* buy me that ring. The "old" dad might have, but we've gotten past that stage now. He'd probably just give me a hard time about it, like Mom.

Mom looked at me doubtfully. "Well, whether he's still spoiling you or not, the answer remains the same for me. I will not buy you that ring."

"Fine!" I said. "That's just *fine.*" I jumped up from the couch. "Who cares about a stupid old ring, anyway?" Now *I* was upset. "Are we done cleaning?" I asked.

"I can do the rest, I guess," Mom answered. "Why? Did you have plans?"

"I didn't," I answered. "But I'm about to make some."

That pleasant Saturday morning had turned into a total drag. Suddenly I needed to get away from my mom for a while. I headed for the phone to call my friends and see if anybody wanted to go to the mall.

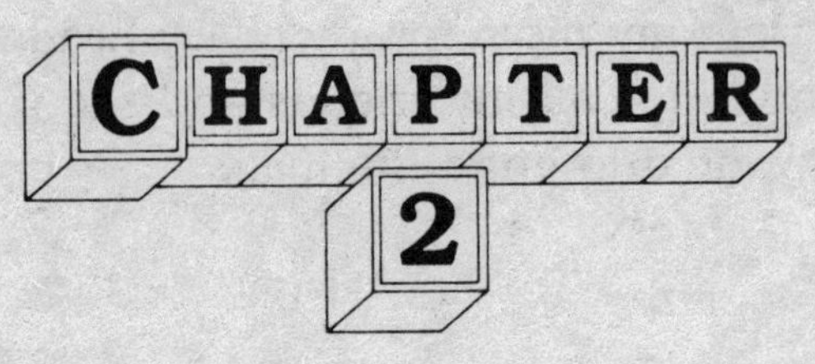

I decided to call Kristy first. If she wanted to go to the mall, there was a good chance that she could talk her brother Charlie into driving us there.

Kristy Thomas is the president of that club I was telling you about, the Baby-sitters Club. She's a good friend; in fact, all the members are my good friends. That's one of the reasons I love the club so much.

As I dialed Kristy's number, I tried to guess who would answer the phone at her house. I often do that when I call her, just because it's a challenging game; the phone could get picked up by any one of about twenty people.

Well, maybe not quite twenty. But Kristy does have a big — and interesting — family.

First there's her mom, who was divorced just like my mom. Only her divorce happened a long time ago, when Kristy's dad up and left the family. At that point, the "family" was

Kristy and her older brothers, Sam and Charlie, plus her little brother, David Michael, who was just a baby at the time. (To keep you up to date, David Michael's seven now, Sam is fifteen, and Charlie is seventeen.)

Mrs. Thomas did a great job of holding her family together after Mr. Thomas left — and it wasn't always easy. Then, not long ago, she met Watson Brewer and ended up getting married again.

Who's Watson Brewer? Well, he's a real, true millionaire — and also a pretty nice guy. Kristy was lucky to get him for a stepfather. And along with Watson, she got a couple of stepsiblings: Karen, who just turned seven, and Andrew, who's four. They live with their mom (Watson's ex-wife) most of the time, but Kristy loves the time they spend with their father — every other weekend and certain vacations. Karen and Andrew are great kids.

When Mrs. Thomas and Watson got married, the family became so big that it made sense for them to move into Watson's mansion — that's right, I said *mansion* — across town. But I guess once they got into the mansion, Watson and Kristy's mom decided that there was too much space left over and they needed to make the family even bigger.

That's when they adopted this little Vietnamese girl they named Emily Michelle. She is *the* cutest two-year-old you've ever seen. Soon after she arrived, Watson and Kristy's mom realized they'd need help taking care of her, so they invited Kristy's grandmother, Nannie, to come live with them too. Whew! I guess it's a full house — or mansion — now. Especially when you take Boo-Boo (that's Watson's mean old cat) and Shannon (David Michael's puppy) into account.

Anyway, this time when I called Kristy's, guess who answered! Kristy herself, for once. She thought the mall was a great idea, and she told me to call everybody else while she talked Charlie into giving us a ride.

It might sound like Kristy was being a little bossy, and maybe she was. But that's just the way she is. Kristy is what teachers call a "good leader." She's always having great ideas, and she knows how to get people to help her put them into action. She's kind of like a grown-up in that way, although it's funny because in other ways she can be immature.

She doesn't care much about makeup or boys or that kind of stuff, and she still dresses like a kid: jeans, turtlenecks, sneakers. She doesn't fool around with her hair, either.

Kristy is pretty short — in fact, she's the shortest girl in our class — so she even looks a little younger than the rest of us. And I guess you'd call her a tomboy. For example, she coaches a softball team made up of little kids. That's Kristy.

I decided to follow her "orders" and call the others, starting with my best friend Claudia. Claudia Kishi is the coolest dresser and most exotic-looking girl in eighth grade. She's exotic-looking because she's Japanese-American, with brown almond-shaped eyes, a gorgeous complexion, and long, thick black hair. She's the coolest dresser because she's not afraid to try new things, and because she is so creative.

Claudia's an artist — she can draw, paint, make sculptures, and do any other kind of art better than anyone I know. She spends a lot of her time and energy on her art, a lot more than she does on her schoolwork, that's for sure. Claud isn't much of a student. Not that she isn't smart. She *is* smart, even though she isn't a certified genius like her older sister Janine. Claus just doesn't care as much about school stuff as she does about art.

Claud has a couple of other passions, ones that her parents don't encourage as much as her artwork. One is Nancy Drew books: She loves to read them even though her parents think they are trash. The other is junk food, which she can't get enough of. She hides her mysteries and her Twinkies, Kit-Kats, and Doritos all over her room.

Claudia was *definitely* up for going to the mall. Next, I called Mary Anne and Dawn.

Mary Anne Spier looks like the "girl next door." She's got brown hair and brown eyes, just like Kristy, and although she has some cool clothes, she's still a pretty conservative dresser. Mary Anne just looks *sweet* — and she is. She's sensitive, and caring, and a really loyal friend. (Such a good friend that she manages to be *best* friends with two people at once: Kristy and Dawn Schafer.)

Mary Anne's mom died when Mary Anne was really young, so her dad was the one to bring her up. Mr. Spier used to be incredibly strict about what Mary Anne could do, and what she could wear. He even had rules about how she could fix her hair. (And I'm not talking about Mary Anne wanting a Mohawk or pink hair. She had to struggle for years just to get her hair out of braids.)

Mr. Spier has finally loosened up, though. He let Mary Anne change her hair and her clothes, allowed her to get a kitten (a gray one, named Tigger), and eased up on the rules and regulations.

I think that when Mr. Spier loosened up, he also realized he was ready for some changes in his own life. Like falling in love and getting married! Mr. Spier got married again to his old high-school sweetheart, who just happened to be the mother of Dawn Schafer, another club member and, as I mentioned before, one of Mary Anne's two best friends.

Here's how it happened: Dawn's mother grew up in Stoneybrook, but then she moved to California, got married, and had two kids (Dawn and her younger brother Jeff, who's now ten). When she got divorced, she moved back to Stoneybrook with Dawn and Jeff. Dawn and Mary Anne became friends at school, and discovered — by looking through old high-school yearbooks — that their parents had once dated! And when Mrs. Schafer and Mr. Spier got together again, the rest was history. Now Mary Anne and her father and Tigger live with Dawn and her mom in an old, old farmhouse that's big enough for all of them. Dawn's brother Jeff doesn't live there, because it turned out he missed California and his dad so much that he was miserable in Stoneybrook. So Jeff moved back out West to live with his father.

Dawn, our California girl, has long, pale blonde hair, blue eyes, and a great sense of style that lets her look very casual and very cool all at once. Dawn is her own person, and she goes her own way, not caring much what other people think of her. I admire her for that.

The main thing Dawn likes about Stoneybrook (besides the Baby-sitters Club, which we invited her to join) is that she can get tofu here. It's a staple of her incredibly healthy diet. And the main thing she dislikes about it is — guess what — *winter.* Dawn's never become convinced that ice-skating and snowball fights fall under the classification of "fun." Beaches are fun. Roller-skating on a boardwalk is fun. But anything you do in below-freezing weather, according to Dawn, cannot be fun.

Mary Anne answered the phone at their house and said she would love to go to the mall. She wanted to stop at the pet store and buy a new toy for Tigger. (Boy, is that kitten spoiled.) Dawn wanted to go, too, even though she didn't really have anything she needed to shop for.

My next call was to Mallory Pike, one of the two younger members of the club. (The other one is Jessica Ramsey.) Mallory may be younger than the rest of us (she and Jessi are eleven and in the sixth grade), but she's really pretty mature. I think she's had to grow up fast because she's the oldest in a *huge* family. Early on, her parents needed her help with the younger kids. All seven of them!

Mal has *seven* younger brothers and sisters, ranging in age from ten (those are the triplets: Adam, Byron and Jordan) down to five (that's Claire). In between, there's Vanessa (she's nine), Nicky (eight), and Margo (seven). So Mal's been baby-sitting for a long, long time.

The frustrating thing for Mallory these days is that even though her parents give her a lot of responsibility, they aren't quite ready to let her grow up. Mal would like to get contacts instead of having to wear glasses, and she would like to wear her red hair in a cooler style, and dress in wilder clothes. But so far, the most her parents have let her do is get her ears pierced. They say the rest will have to wait until she's older, so Mal just has to be patient.

While she's waiting, Mal entertains herself with fantasies of becoming a children's book author/illustrator. She loves to write and draw, and she's good at both things, so don't be surprised if you see her name on a book jacket someday. Mal also has fantasies of being a horse owner. She loves to read, and horse stories are her favorites. But the Pikes' house is much too crowded for the golden palomino Mal dreams of.

Mallory's best friend, Jessica Ramsey, loves horse books, too. In fact, when I called Mallory, Jessi was over there, sitting in Mal's room reading *Black Beauty* for the thousandth time. Mal was reading one of the Misty books. They both decided to leave the books for awhile, though, and join us at the mall.

Jessi's family is different from Mallory's. She's only got one sister (Becca, who's nine) and one brother (Squirt — that's his nickname — who's just a baby). Plus, the Ramseys are different in another way. They're black. Of course, that isn't a problem for Mal, or for any of us club members, but some people in the neighborhood weren't all that happy when the Ramseys moved in. By now things have gotten better, but they weren't easy in the beginning.

What does Jessi fantasize about? (Besides being thirteen, that is.) Jessi dreams of being a ballerina someday. I'd have to say that her dream is pretty close to reality, too. Jessi's already one of the best dancers in her ballet school in Stamford. She's gotten the lead in more than one major production, and she is really something to see when she's on stage. Jessi is *talented* and she works really hard at her dancing. That's why I think she'll be taking curtain calls in a big New York City theater someday in the future.

I hung up the phone, now that I was done with my calls, and went into my bedroom to change and get ready for the mall. My mom was still vacuuming downstairs, and I wondered if I should make up with her before I left. But then I heard Charlie honk his car horn outside, and I looked out the window to see Kristy motioning to me to hurry. So instead of making up, I just told my mom where I was going and gave her a wave as I ran out of the house. I was really looking forward to spending the day at the mall with my friends.

"Hey, guys," I said, as I climbed into the backseat. "Thank you for driving us, Charlie."

"No big deal," he answered. "I was going to the mall anyway to see a movie with some of the guys."

"And to check out the girls, too," said Kristy. "Right?"

Charlie turned red. I thought maybe I should change the subject. "Isn't the Junk Bucket running?" I asked him. The Junk Bucket is Charlie's car, and it's a pretty good name for the clattery old thing. But that day, Charlie wasn't driving his car. We were riding along in true luxury, in Watson's station wagon.

"It's running," he said. "But just barely. Watson said I could take his car today since he wasn't using it."

We stopped to pick up Dawn and Mary Anne, and they squeezed in next to me.

"Mmmm," I said. "Somebody smells good. What is that smell?"

"Must be my new shampoo," answered Dawn. "It's called 'Wildflower Wash.' " She tossed her hair, and I could smell the sweet scent again.

Charlie coughed. "Smells more like 'Accident in the Perfume Factory' to me," he said. We all cracked up.

Jessi and Mal were waiting at the Pikes' house, sitting on the porch with the triplets. "Can't we go, too?" pleaded Byron.

"Sorry," said Jessi. "Girls only."

"But Charlie's a boy," said Adam.

"Girls and *grown-up* boys only," said Mal. "Sorry, guys. Maybe another time."

"That's what you always say," muttered Jordan.

Mal and Jessi waved at the boys and ran to the car. Since it was getting pretty crowded, they decided to curl up in the way back. They looked like a couple of little kids there, giggling as they wiggled into comfortable positions.

The last stop was at Claudia's. She ran out as soon as we honked, dressed in her current favorite mall outfit. Claud looked terrific in black leggings, red high-top sneakers, and an oversized red sweater. She was carrying a red plastic lunch box as a purse. Claudia jumped into the front seat with Kristy, and we were on our way.

When we pulled into the mall's parking lot, we couldn't see any empty spaces. Charlie groaned. "Seems like this is the place to be today," he said, as he drove up and down the lanes. "Oh, here's one," he said finally.

"Charlie," said Kristy, once he'd pulled into the space. "We must be about two miles away from the mall. I can barely see Sears from here!"

"I told you I'd get you here, and I did," Charlie answered. "Want me to call you a taxi to take you the rest of the way?"

"Oh, ha, ha," said Kristy. "No, thanks. I think we'll be able to walk it in an hour or two."

"Good," said Charlie. "Listen, I've gotta go. I'm supposed to meet the guys in five minutes. How about if we meet at Mr. Pretzel at four o'clock?"

We agreed that that sounded fine. "Bye, Charlie," called Kristy. "And thanks!" Charlie ran across the parking lot. "I bet it's not 'the guys' he's meeting," said Kristy. "He seems to be in a real hurry, if you know what I mean." We all giggled.

When we pushed open the doors of the mall, I stood for a minute and took a deep breath. I love the way the mall smells — like new shoes and cookies baking and pizza hot out of the oven and perfume and, well, just a lot of good smells mixed together.

The place was packed. Groups of kids were hanging out on every corner. Mothers and fathers pushed strollers and dragged whining toddlers from store to store. Couples walked along with their hands in each other's back pockets, smiling at each other as if nobody else existed.

In the store windows were bright signs, and mannequins dressed in cool (and probably very expensive) clothes. Silver balloons floated from stalls in the middle of the main walkway. Music blared from the record store. The fountain in the center of the mall shot a spray of pink water high into the air.

I love the mall.

We sat down on the edge of the fountain, which is one of the cool places to hang out, and started to plan our afternoon. Mary Anne couldn't wait to go to the pet store, and Jessi and Mal said they'd go there, too.

"I love to look at the puppies," said Mal.

"I know," said Jessi with a sigh. "Except I always feel so bad that I can't take them home with me. They look so sad in their little cages."

Claudia said she'd pass on looking at the animals. "I want to check out this new line of sneakers I saw in a magazine," she said. "They look pretty outrageous."

"Sounds good to me," I said. "I don't have much money to spend, but I'm always up for looking at shoes."

Dawn wanted to window-shop, too, but Kristy voted to stick with Mary Ann. So we ended up splitting into two groups, and we agreed to meet at the pet store in an hour.

"Before we do anything else," said Claudia as soon as we were on our way, "we've *got* to stop for nachos. I'm starving."

I wasn't interested in nachos (I have to be really careful about what kind of junk food I eat), but I didn't mind stopping at the Tortilla Queen place, and neither did Dawn. See, this really cute guy works there. . . .

But it must have been his day off. There was no sign of him at the counter, just this greasy-looking bald guy who appeared incredibly bored. We sat by the window while Claud ate her nachos, watching the crowds go by. I love see what people are wearing at the mall — everything from ripped jeans to fur coats.

"Okay," said Claud, wiping her fingers with a napkin. "Now where should we go?"

We walked slowly down one side of the mall, stopping in whatever stores looked like fun. Dawn loves the T-shirt store, so we spent some time in there. She tried to decide between a blue shirt with a picture of whales on it and a yellow one that said "Go For It" in big black letters, but she finally ended up getting neither. "I don't really *need* a new T-shirt right now," she said.

"I don't really *need* new sneakers, either," said Claud. "But that's not going to stop me!" She led the way to the shoe store. Claud has the biggest sneaker collection of anyone I know, I swear. She's got red ones (two other pairs besides the ones she was wearing that day) and purple ones and black ones and white ones and polka-dotted ones. I bet she could wear a different pair of sneakers every day for a month.

"What do you think?" she asked, holding up a pair of lace-and-sequin-trimmed pink high-tops. "Pretty cool, right?"

I knew from looking through that month's

magazines that those shoes were past cool. "Nice," I said. "Can you afford them?"

"Sure. I don't need any new art supplies right now, and I'm sure I'll be sitting a lot this month, so there's no need to save the money I've got." She asked the clerk for a size seven, and tried them on. "I love them," she told him, as she checked herself in the mirror.

While Claudia was paying for the sneakers, Dawn and I watched two women try on high heels. The funny thing was that both of them pretended they had the tiniest, most delicate feet. They started out asking the clerk for "size six, please," but they ended up working their way to "size nine and a half, I guess" before they could squeeze their feet into the shoes.

Dawn and I were nearly dying with held-in laughter by the time we made it out of the store. We exploded as soon as we'd gotten through the door. " 'Oh, well, size twelve ought to do it,' " said Dawn, imitating one woman. " 'But I'm a *small* size twelve, mind you.' "

Tears were running down my cheeks from laughing so hard. We walked past a few more stores, laughing again every time we thought about the women, and then we reached the pet shop.

Mary Anne had bought a catnip mouse for Tigger. When we arrived, she and the others were gazing lovingly at the puppies and kittens that were for sale.

"Isn't he *adorable*?" asked Jessi, pointing at a black Labrador retriever puppy. He was a pretty cute dog, I had to admit.

"Look at this one," said Kristy, dragging me over to see a bulldog puppy in another cage. "Isn't he something?"

"He's something, all right," I answered. "If you happen to like squashed faces!"

After the pet store, we went to Friendly's for ice cream. At least, the others had ice cream. I ate a tuna sandwich, and it tasted great. I wasn't even envious of Claud's Hot Fudge Brownie Delite. Well, not *too* envious, anyway.

We didn't have to meet Charlie for another half hour, so after Friendly's, so we decided to cruise up the other side of the mall. As we were walking, I spotted something in the window of Town and Country Jewelry. A birthstone ring display! I came to a complete stop and looked closer, the others crowding behind me. The diamond ring was beautiful — a circle of diamonds in a gold setting — but it cost a *lot* more than the other one I'd seen.

I told everybody how much I wanted a ring like that, and about the fight I'd had that morning with my mom. Claud bent closer to look at the price of the ring. "Wow!" she said. "I've never had a piece of jewelry that cost anything like that."

"I wouldn't *dare* to ask my parents for a diamond ring," said Mallory. "Even if it was my birthstone."

"But it *is* totally gorgeous, don't you think?" I asked.

Everybody nodded, but they looked a little overwhelmed. I wished they could have been more on my side. I wanted Claud to say, "You deserve a ring like that, Stacey, and your mother's a meanie not to buy it for you." But she didn't say that.

Still, when I got home that night, I couldn't resist bringing up the subject again with my mother. She seemed to be in a good mood — she'd forgotten our fight, obviously — so I decided to go for it. I described the ring I'd seen that day, and then I told her how much it cost. "So the one at Stoneybrook Jewelers is really a bargain in comparison," I said, figuring that she'd be convinced by my logical argument.

"Stacey," she replied, "you don't seem to

understand. The answer is no. Absolutely not. I am not buying a diamond ring for you."

What could I say? Nothing. Instead, I headed upstairs to call Claudia and complain about my hard-hearted mom.

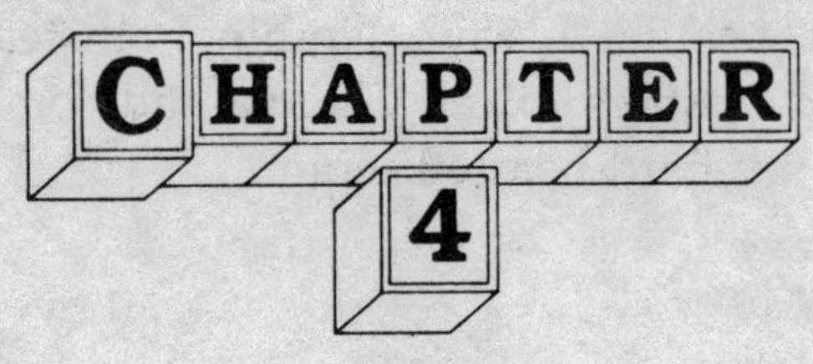

By Monday afternoon, when I went to Claud's house for our club meeting, I was feeling a little better. I'd decided to forget about the ring, since it seemed that I wasn't going to get it. My mom had made her feelings clear, and you know what? I didn't even want to ask my dad. It's true that he sometimes spoils me. Then my mom gets mad, and I feel in the middle again. Who needs that?

I reached Claud's room early, and she and Kristy were the only ones there so far. Claud was there because we meet in her room, and Kristy was there because Kristy likes to be punctual. Kristy was sitting where she usually sits. In the director's chair. She was wearing her visor, and she'd stuck a pencil over one ear. Ready for action.

Claud was sitting cross-legged on her bed, a sketch pad balanced on her knees. She was looking up at Kristy and then down at the paper. Her charcoal made quick scratchy lines. Then she rubbed the paper to blend them in. I sat next to her on the bed and looked at the drawing. "Hey, that's really good!" I said. I don't know why I was surprised. I know my best friend is a great artist. But this picture just looked so — so *Kristyish.* I couldn't even put my finger on why it looked so much like her. Was it her nose? Her hair? The way she was leaning in the chair? I don't know. It was just Kristy, there on the paper.

"Almost time to start," said Kristy, as Mary Anne and Dawn walked in. They plopped down on the bed, too.

"Great picture!" said Dawn.

"Thanks," replied Claud. "But look at these hands. I'd better go wash up." She held out her hands to show us how filthy they were. They were smudged and blackened with charcoal.

As soon as Claud left the room, Kristy grabbed the sketch. "This really looks like me?" she asked. We nodded. She studied the drawing closely. When Claud came back in, Kristy asked if she could keep the picture.

"Sure," said Claudia. "It's yours."

Mallory walked in just then, with Jessi right behind her. They took their usual places on the floor. Kristy passed the picture to them. "That's great!" said Mal. "Would you do me some time?"

At that moment, I saw the digital clock on Claud's night table flip to 5:30. "Order!" said Kristy. "Time for the meeting."

As I said, Kristy likes to be punctual.

Actually, I think it's a good thing that she is so serious about running our club professionally. That way it's more like a business than a club. We have fun, but we also get the job done.

Kristy opens the meetings because she's the president. And she's the president because starting the club was her idea. None of us had thought of a baby-sitters club before Kristy. She's good at coming up with new ideas — ideas that really work.

Kristy got the idea for the club back in seventh grade. That was before her mom married Watson, so Kristy still lived on Bradford Court, right across the street from Claudia. Anyway, Kristy used to baby-sit for her little brother, David Michael, after school, and also whenever her mom wanted to go out in the evening. If Kristy had other plans, Charlie or Sam would take over.

But one night, everybody was busy and Mrs. Thomas decided she'd have to call a sitter. She was on the phone for about an hour, calling everybody she could think of, but nobody could take the job. She was getting more and more frustrated, but Kristy, watching her, was becoming excited.

She'd had an idea.

What if her mom could make one phone call that would put her in touch with a whole bunch of experienced sitters? This would have saved her a lot of time and energy, and she would have been guaranteed a sitter. The next day Kristy told Claudia and Mary Anne about her idea, and they saw right away how well it could work. But they thought that three girls weren't enough, so Claud suggested inviting me to join, too. (My family had just moved to Stoneybrook, and Claud and I had started to become friends.) Then when Dawn moved to Stoneybrook, she joined, too.

The club worked perfectly from the beginning. We've always met in Claud's room, between 5:30 and 6:00 every Monday, Wednesday, and Friday. Why Claud's room? Because she has her very own phone, with a private line. By using her number for our club, we avoid tying up any adults' phones. Since we use her room and her phone, Claud was made vice president.

Anyway, while we're meeting, parents can call and arrange for whatever sitting jobs they need. How do they know to call? Well, by now our business is mostly advertised by word of mouth — parents telling other parents — but at first we got the word out by distributing fliers. Once in a while we still pass them out, if we feel we need extra business. The fliers tell about the club and tell parents when and where to call.

You might be wondering when Jessi and Mal joined the club. Well, that was during the time my family left Stoneybrook to move back to New York. The club had so much business that my friends decided they needed more members, and Jessi and Mal were perfect candidates. Luckily, when I returned to Stoneybrook, there was no question that I would be able to join again, too.

What's my job in the club? I'm the treasurer. That means I keep track of how much money we earn. We each get to keep whatever money we make, but it's interesting to know the total amount. I also get to collect dues, which I was about to do that very minute.

"It's Monday," I said, when Kristy asked whether there was any club business. "You all know what *that* means!" I had a big smile on my face but everybody else was frowning. They hate to part with their money but I just love to collect it. I like to keep our manila envelope fat with money in case of an emergency.

Of course, we don't often have emergencies, so the money is spent on other things. Like paying Charlie to drive Kristy to meetings, now that she no longer lives across the street from "headquarters." And for pizza parties or sleepover snacks. And for —

"Stacey," said Dawn suddenly. I realized I'd been daydreaming. "I need some new markers for my Kid-Kit. Is there enough money?"

Kid-Kits. That's just what I was going to tell you about. Kid-Kits are boxes that we've decorated to look cool. Inside, we put books and crayons and stickers and toys that kids love. The kits were another of Kristy's ideas when she noticed that kids always seem to like *other* kids' toys better than their own. Most of the stuff in our kits isn't new, but it is different. The kits help to make us popular sitters!

I counted out some money and handed it to Dawn. "Is that enough?" I asked.

"Sure," she said. "If I want to buy two markers!" She made a face at me. "Come on, Stacey. You can spare a little more."

I dug out two more dollars. "Okay?" I said. Dawn nodded. I heard some giggling, but I ignored it. Everybody thinks I'm stingy, but I'm just protecting *their* better interests. If I didn't watch every penny, there wouldn't be money in the treasury when we need it.

"Jessi," said Kristy just then, "I noticed that you didn't write up your last job in the club notebook."

"Oh, that's right. I'm sorry," said Jessi. "I didn't have time because I had an extra dance class this week. I'll do it right now." She reached for the book.

The club notebook is where we record all the jobs we go on each week. Once again, this was Kristy's idea — and it's not one of her more popular ones. It takes a lot of time to do all that writing. Plus, we have to read the new entries in the notebook every week. But I guess it's worth it. When we read the notebook, we stay up-to-date with what's going on with our clients. And sometimes there are really good sitting ideas in there, like new games to play on rainy afternoons and stuff like that.

While Jessi was writing up her job, the

phone rang. We all dived for it, but I was the one to grab first. "Hello?" I said. It was Mrs. Rodowsky, calling to see if one of us could sit for her three sons the next afternoon. I told her I'd call her back.

Mary Anne checked the record book to see who was available. She's our club secretary, and she does a terrific job of keeping track of our schedules — Claud's art classes, my doctor appointments, Jessi's dance lessons, and all. If she tells you that, for example, Kristy is the only one free on a Thursday afternoon, you can be sure she's right. Mary Anne has never once made a mistake. Within two minutes I was able to call Mrs. Rodowsky back and tell her that Mal would be her sitter.

You may be wondering what jobs Dawn, Jessi, and Mal have. Well, Dawn is what we call the alternate officer. That means that she is prepared to take over for any of us if we can't make a meeting. She did my job as treasurer the whole time I was back in New York, and she was good at it, too. But I don't think she enjoyed it the way I do, so Dawn was happy to give the position to me when I returned.

Jessi and Mal are what we call junior officers, which means that they can't sit at night for anybody except their own siblings. It's great to have them working in the afternoons, since that frees up the rest of us to sit in the evenings.

What do we do if none of us can take a job? Well, that's where our associate members come in. We have two of them, Shannon Kilbourne and Logan Bruno. They don't come to meetings, but when we need them we can call on them. Shannon lives in Kristy's new neighborhood, and she goes to a private school, so none of us knows her too well. She seems nice, though. And Logan — well, guess what. Logan is Mary Anne's boyfriend! They've been having some problems lately (they even broke up for a while), but we do see them together a lot. Logan is a great guy and a good sitter. We're lucky he's in the club.

Our meeting that day went quickly. Then, just as we were getting ready to break up, we received one last phone call. Kristy answered it, and talked for a while. When she hung up, she told us we had a new client! Her name was Mrs. Gardella (Claud was the only one who'd ever heard of her — Mrs. Gardella knew Claudia's mom from the library where Mrs. Kishi works) and Kristy thought she must be pretty rich. That was because the Gardellas had a full-time nanny to take care of their baby! But now the nanny had to go away for a few weeks ("family troubles," said Mrs. Gardella), and the Gardellas desperately needed a sitter for Tara, Mouse, and Bird on Friday night. Mrs. Gardella had heard "absolutely wonderful" things about our club from her friends and neighbors.

"Mouse and Bird?" asked Dawn.

"The cat and dog," said Kristy, raising her eyebrows and shrugging.

"How old is Tara?" I asked.

"Seven months," answered Kristy.

I looked at Mary Anne, who was checking the record book, and crossed my fingers. I love to sit for babies, and I was really hoping that I'd get the job. When Mary Anne glanced up, she looked straight at me. "Looks like you've got it," she said. "You're the only one free on Friday night."

All right! New clients — and a baby. Suddenly I couldn't wait for Friday.

I have to admit that by Friday I was a little nervous about my job at the Gardellas'. I always feel that way the first time I sit for a new client, because there's so much I don't know. What will their house be like? Are they nice? Will the kids be angels — or monsters? Will the parents give out the information I need, or will I have to remember to ask all the right questions?

I thought about that stuff as I walked to their house. In fact, I was so deep in thought that I almost missed the black wrought-iron fence and gate that Mrs. Gardella had told me to watch for. "Just make sure to latch the gate behind you when you come in," she'd said. "I wouldn't want Bird to go into the street."

Now that I saw the house, I remembered walking by it before. But I never thought I'd be going into it. It was a pretty impressive house: brick, with big white columns on either side of the humongous front door. A white urn stood to the right of the door, spilling over with ivy and red flowers. I opened the gate, and then carefully closed it behind me. I didn't see any dogs in the yard, but I figured it was better not to take chances. Then I walked up the brick pathway and stood on the porch, looking for the doorbell.

I couldn't find it. Was I going to have to stand out there until somebody happened to open the door?

Finally, I saw this thing in the middle of the door: it was brass, and shaped kind of like a music-box key. Could that be the doorbell? I reached out and gave the key a turn. Brrrring! Yup, that was it.

Immediately after the bell rang, a dog started barking ferociously. I looked through the little windows on either side of the door, and saw this huge black dog — with huge yellowish teeth! Now, I'm not usually afraid of dogs, but this one looked mean. I stepped back from the window, but the dog kept on barking.

"All *right*, Bird," I heard a woman's voice say. "That's enough! Go lie down."

The door opened. "Mrs. Gardella?" I said. "I'm — "

Just then the dog pushed his head into the open door, squeezed past Mrs. Gardella, and jumped up on me.

"Oh!" I said, surprised. For a second I was scared, but then I noticed that the dog was wagging his tail and, instead of trying to bite me, he was licking my face. "Nice dog," I said.

"Bird!" exclaimed Mrs. Gardella. "Down, boy!" She grabbed his collar. "I'm so sorry," she said. "He's just too friendly, that's his problem. I keep trying to train him not to do that, but my husband actually *likes* the dog to jump up on him, so I think Bird is confused."

"It's okay," I said. I reached out to Bird. Mrs. Gardella was still holding his collar, so I figured it was safe to pat him. "Hi, Bird," I said, stroking his head. "Good dog."

"Now, you must be Tracy, right?" asked Mrs. Gardella.

"Um, that's *Stacey*," I said. I hate having to correct adults. "Stacey McGill."

"I'm sorry, Stacey," she said. "I'm terrible with names. Now, let's see. I'm ready to go but Mr. Gardella is still dressing, so why don't I show you around?"

I forgot to tell you what Mrs. Gardella was wearing. She was pretty dressed up — definitely more dressed up than most parents I sit for. I guess she and her husband were going to a formal party. Mrs. Gardella was wearing this tight black dress made of velvet, with a low back and long sleeves. Her shoes were velvet, too, with really high heels. She had on a diamond necklace and diamond earrings, and her black hair was pulled back with a diamond clip.

I didn't mean to stare.

"Pretty fancy, right?" Mrs. Gardella said, when she caught me looking. "We're going to a party at my husband's boss's house, and it's going to be dressy. So I got out all the family jewels." She smiled.

She was nice. Even though she was rich, she was just a regular person. Already I liked her.

"Now," she said. "Where shall we start?" She led the way through the main hall and into a huge living room stuffed with fancy furniture and expensive-looking lamps. A grand piano stood in one corner, a beautiful red silk scarf on top of it.

On top of the scarf sat a cat.

I thought Mrs. Gardella would be upset about the cat sitting on that beautiful polished piano, lounging around on a piece of priceless material. But no.

"Oh, here he is," she said, walking to the cat and picking him up. "You've met Bird, now meet Mouse. How's my little Mousie?" She cooed, hugging him to her chest. His fluffy coat was leaving little white hairs all over her fancy dress, but she didn't seem to care.

"Um, hi, Mouse," I said. I wasn't sure how to talk to a cat. "He's pretty," I said to Mrs. Gardella.

"Isn't he?" she asked. Just then I felt something wet pushing my hand. I almost jumped out of my skin! But when I looked down, I saw that it was only Bird, poking his nose around as if to say, "Pat me!"

"Oh, Bird is jealous," said Mrs. Gardella. "You'll have to be careful about that. Whenever you give one of them attention, make sure to be fair to the other one, too. Otherwise they pick up on it and get angry and hurt."

I nodded and patted Bird.

"Now, let me show you where their food is," Mrs. Gardella continued, "and I'll tell you all about their dinner routine. They're used to having things done a certain way, and they get upset if their routine is disrupted." She led the way to the kitchen.

I walked behind her. I was beginning to think that she was just a little bit strange. She was talking about her pets as if they were children — and I hadn't even met the *real* baby.

"Tara's taking a late nap," Mrs. Gardella called over her shoulder, as if she'd read my mind. "I'll wake her before we leave, and then she'll be up for a couple of hours. She's such a good baby. I don't think you'll have any trouble with her at all."

She showed me around the kitchen, explaining what each of the pets should be given for dinner. No canned food for *these* animals! Bird was having hamburger mixed with rice, and Mouse would be dining on chicken livers.

"Be sure to take the food out of the fridge half an hour or so before you feed them," she said. "If the food is too cold it will upset their stomachs."

She showed me Bird's bowl. It sat in the corner of their fancy dining room, placed on a little oriental rug.

"And where does Mouse eat?" I asked.

"Oh, Mousie usually joins us at the table," she said, pointing.

I looked at the huge, highly polished table. Sure enough, a small silver dish sat in the center of the table, between two fancy candlesticks. "He's been eating with us ever since he was a kitten, and I just can't bear to make him stop now."

After the kitchen/dining room tour, Mrs. Gardella led me back into the living room to show me how to entertain Mouse and Bird. (She didn't seem to be worried about what I would do with Tara!) "This is Bird's favorite toy," she said, holding up a plastic hamburger. "He loves the way it squeaks." She squeezed it a couple of times, and Bird came running. Then she threw it gently across the room and he raced off after it, skidding over the big rugs and almost bashing into a glass-fronted cabinet.

Mrs. Gardella laughed. "Isn't he funny?" she asked. "He just loves to retrieve things. He'll do it as long as somebody will keep throwing his toy."

"That's because he's a *bird* dog. He's bred to retrieve things," said a deep voice behind me. I turned around to see a man in a tuxedo. "Hi, I'm Mr. Gardella," he said.

"I'm Stacey," I answered.

"I guess you've got the rundown on these two, right?" he said.

"Yup. I think we'll have a fine time."

"I just have to wake Tara, honey," said Mrs. Gardella. "Then we can go." I followed her upstairs and into the baby's room. Tara was asleep in her crib. I looked around the room while Mrs. Gardella woke her up. It was adorable! Everything was pink and white, with a rosebud theme. Her crib, her dresser, her changing table; everything matched. Even the lampshade and the wallpaper matched.

"Hi, sweetie," I heard Mrs. Gardella coo to the baby. "Time to wake up and meet Stacey." She held Tara up to see me. Tara giggled and stared at me with big blue eyes. She seemed like a happy baby, and I said so to Mrs. Gardella.

"Oh, she is!" she replied. "She is *such* a happy girl, and such a good girl. I know you two will have fun together." She handed the baby to me and checked her makeup in the rosebud-trimmed mirror.

"Kay!" shouted Mr. Gardella from downstairs. "We're going to be late."

"Coming!"

Carrying Tara, I followed Mrs. Gardella downstairs. She and her husband took turns kissing the baby good-bye, and then they made a big scene over the pets.

"You be a good, good boy," said Mr. Gardella to Bird while Mrs. Gardella gave Mouse one last hug. "Come up and say good-bye," he added, patting his chest to show Bird what he wanted. Bird jumped up, put his front paws on Mr. Gardella's chest, and licked his face.

"Oh, Peter," said Mrs. Gardella. "Now you've got paw prints on your white shirt."

"Well, we match. You've got cat hair all over your dress," he answered. They laughed as they headed out the door.

I shook my head. Then I looked down at Tara. "Are you hungry?" I asked. Bird's ears perked up at the word "hungry," and Mouse started to rub against my ankles. "Okay, I guess we're all hungry," I said. "Let's get some dinner."

It took me a while to get used to eating at such a big fancy table, especially this particular big fancy table, with a cat sitting in the middle of it, calmly eating chicken livers out of a silver bowl. But the dinner went smoothly, and so did the rest of the evening.

I put Tara to bed after we'd played for a while in the living room, and then I played with Mouse and Bird. Bird mainly wanted to be scratched behind the ears, and Mouse seemed to enjoy batting his toys under the couch and then waiting for me to "rescue" them.

By the time the Gardellas came home, I was pretty tired. I felt as if I'd been sitting for three kids!

"Did Mouse eat all his dinner?" Mrs. Gardella asked, just seconds after they'd walked in the door.

"Was Bird a good boy?" asked Mr. Gardella.

I answered their questions while they said hello to Mouse and Bird, who seemed overjoyed to see them. Then Mrs. Gardella finally asked about the baby. "Did Tara get back to sleep all right?" she said.

"She was fine," I answered. "She's a wonderful baby." Then Mr. Gardella paid me (and gave me a pretty good tip) and drove me home. I had enjoyed the evening. But I couldn't help thinking that the Gardellas were a little bit weird. Really, really nice — but definitely weird.

"Stacey." I heard someone calling my name. I tried to answer, but it was as if I were underwater; no sound came out. "Stacey, wake up!" the voice said again.

It was my mother. I struggled to wake up. My bed was so cozy, and I was snuggled down into it so comfortably. I opened one eye and looked at the clock next to my bed. Eight o'clock. Oh, no! I was going to be late for school.

Then I remembered it was Saturday. I relaxed. There was no rush. I let my eyes close again. "Stacey! Didn't you hear me call?" My mother was now standing at my bedroom door, looking a little impatient.

"What is it?" I asked. I love to sleep late on weekends, and my mom knows that. Because she's always worrying about my health (ever since I got diabetes, that is), she lets me sleep pretty much as late as I want. In fact, she always says that she hates to wake me when I can sleep in. So why was she waking me?

"There's a phone call for you," she said.

"Please tell whomever it is that I'll call back," I answered. "I'm not ready to get up." I figured it was Claud, wanting to know what my plans were for the day.

"Stacey," said my mother, "it's Mrs. Gardella. And she wants to speak to you right away."

I sat up in bed. All of a sudden I was completely awake. "Mrs. Gardella?" I asked.

"Yes," answered my mom. "And she sounds upset."

I got up and scrambled into my robe and slippers. I was still tying the belt to my robe as I headed for the phone. Mrs. Gardella! Ordinarily I'd be mad if somebody called me so early on a Saturday and interrupted my delicious extra sleep. But this call made me worried, not angry. Had I done something wrong with Tara last night? Was she sick? Or was Mouse or Bird? Or had one of them done something terrible that I should have noticed?

My heart was pounding as I grabbed the phone. "Hello?" I said.

"Stacey, this is Mrs. Gardella."

"Hi," I said. "Is Tara okay?"

"She's fine — "

"What about Mouse? And Bird?" I asked, interrupting her.

"They're fine, too," she said. Then she paused. "But — but my jewelry isn't."

Her jewelry? I didn't know what she was talking about. Did she mean all those diamonds she was wearing the night before? I didn't say anything, because I didn't know what to say.

"Well," she continued, "I don't mean *all* my jewelry. Just the one ring. My diamond. It's missing, and I'm very upset about it."

"Diamond ring?" I repeated, sounding (I realized later) pretty dumb.

"Yes," she said. "It's a gold band, studded with little diamonds. I set it out on my dresser last night because I was going to wear it."

"Uh-huh," I said.

"And I guess I forgot to put it on, because you rang the bell just as I had finished dressing," she went on. "Then this morning I discovered that it was gone."

"It's gone?" I still wasn't sounding too smart. "Maybe it rolled off the dresser."

"We've looked everywhere. Peter — I mean, Mr. Gardella — has practically turned the house upside down. We just can't find it anywhere."

Suddenly, a light switched on in my head. Was she going to accuse me —

"I hate even to suggest this, Stacey," she said, sounding embarrassed. "But could you possibly have 'borrowed' my ring? Maybe you — maybe you just wanted to show it to your friends. . . . " She obviously felt almost as awkward as I did about the phone call.

"Of course I didn't borrow it!" I said loudly, without thinking. "I mean," I continued, trying to control my voice, "I didn't take your ring, Mrs. Gardella. I didn't even set foot in your bedroom. The only upstairs room I was in was Tara's. I'm sorry your ring is missing, but I promise you that I did not take it."

Mrs. Gardella cleared her throat. "Stacey," she said, "can I please speak to your mother?"

I held the phone away from my ear and looked at it. Wow. She didn't believe me. This was too much. "Mom!" I called.

"What is it?" she said, from right behind me. She must have been standing there listening the whole time. She looked worried.

I didn't feel like explaining any of it. "Mrs. Gardella wants to talk to you," I said, handing her the phone.

She frowned. "Yes?" she said into the receiver.

Then she didn't say anything for a while. Mrs. Gardella must have been explaining the situation to her. Mom just kept nodding. Then, finally, she started talking.

"Mrs. Gardella," she began, "you don't know my daughter very well, or you would know that she's not the kind of girl who would steal anything from one of her clients' houses. Or from anyone's house!"

Then she was quiet again for a moment.

"Well," she said, after the pause, "I can't imagine where the ring is, either, but Stacey isn't a thief — or a liar. I'm sorry you feel that way."

I watched my mother's face closely while she talked. Of course, she must be remembering what I was remembering: the fight we'd had the other day about a diamond ring. She was defending my honor to Mrs. Gardella, but I couldn't help wondering. Was she a little bit suspicious? Did she think that, just maybe, I *could* have stolen that ring?

I felt awful.

Then my mom handed the phone back to me. Her lips were tight. "She wants to speak to you again," she said.

I took the phone. "Hello?"

"Stacey," said Mrs. Gardella, "I don't know how to tell you this. I know you've denied taking the ring, and I understand why your mother feels that she has to defend you."

Of course I denied it. I didn't *do* it.

"But," she went on. "The fact remains that the ring is missing. I can't ignore that."

"Well, I'll understand if you don't want me to sit for you anymore," I said quietly. "But I didn't — "

She cut me off. "It's not just you," she said. "I don't believe I'll be hiring any of the girls from your club anymore."

Oh no!

"And," she continued, "I'm afraid I'm going to have to call your other clients and let them know about this situation. It's only fair that they be warned."

I couldn't believe my ears. "Oh, please don't do that!" I said. "Our club has such a good reputation. Nothing like this has ever happened before."

"But it has happened now," said Mrs. Gardella, "and, as I said, I can't ignore it."

I couldn't think of anything else to say.

"I'm sure you're a very nice girl, Stacey," she said. "But that was an expensive ring, and

I have to take its loss seriously."

The phone call was over. I hung up, feeling like I'd been punched in the stomach. Then I burst into tears.

My mother gave me a big hug. "I don't know what to say," she said. "That woman has her mind made up, hasn't she?"

"Thanks for trying to defend me," I said through my tears.

Mom put her finger under my chin and tilted my face toward hers. "I defended you because I know you would never do such a thing," she said seriously. "I know my daughter. It's just too bad Mrs. Gardella doesn't."

I told my mom what Mrs. Gardella had said. "Do you really think she'll call our other clients?" I asked.

"I hope she waits for a few days," answered Mom. "Maybe if she gives herself a chance to cool down, she'll realize she's made a mistake."

I nodded, sniffing. "I better call Kristy," I said, picking up the phone. I dialed slowly, trying to control myself. Kristy wasn't going to like this one bit.

Sure enough, when I told her about my conversation with Mrs. Gardella, Kristy was furious.

"How *dare* she?" she asked. "I can't believe this."

"I didn't take the ring, Kristy," I said in a small voice.

"Stacey," she answered. "I know and you know that you didn't take the ring. Don't worry about that. But what we *do* have to worry about is keeping the clients that we already have."

"How are we going to do that?" I asked.

"I don't know yet. But I do know that this calls for an emergency meeting of the BSC. Can you make it to Claud's house by noon?"

I told her I could.

"Good," she said. "I'll call everybody else. There must be something we can do."

After we hung up, I went to the bathroom to wash my face. I looked at myself in the mirror. This was serious business, and I knew it. "Stacey McGill," I said to myself, "just remember this: You are not a thief." I nodded firmly. But I felt very, very scared.

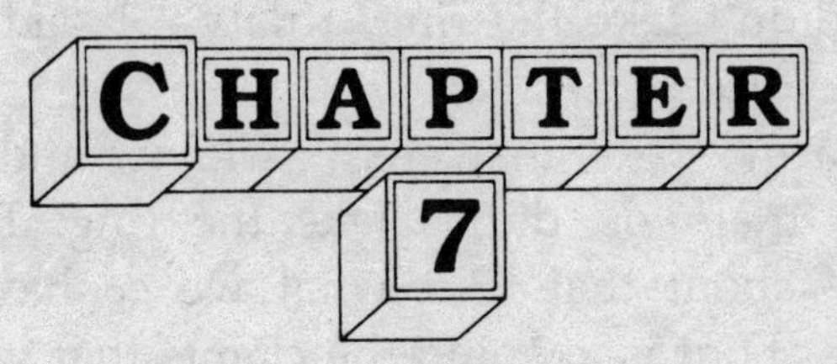

I was late arriving at Claud's. My morning had not gone well after the phone call from Mrs. Gardella. First, when I stepped into the shower, I discovered that I was out of my favorite shampoo. Then I couldn't find any clean clothes to wear. And when I was fixing breakfast, I dropped an egg on the floor.

Then, just to cap everything off, when I tested my blood sugar (something I have to do several times a day), it was high. I adjusted the amount of insulin for my injection, but I would have to have to keep an eye on myself for awhile. Sometimes a high reading doesn't mean much at all, but sometimes it can be a warning sign.

So you can understand why I was feeling a little scattered by the time I got to the meeting.

When I walked in, everybody else was already there. I had heard them talking while I walked up the stairs, but as soon as I opened the door, they became quiet. Had they been talking about me?

"Hi, Stacey," chorused Jessi and Mal. They were sitting on the floor, looking a little nervous.

"Hi, Stacey," said Dawn. She was perched on the bed between Claudia and Mary Anne. The three of them seemed awfully serious.

I said hi, sat down in Claud's desk chair, and turned to look at Kristy, who hadn't said a word yet. She was in the director's chair, as usual. But she *wasn't* wearing her usual "meeting smile." In fact, she looked very, very grim.

I felt pretty grim myself.

I knew that since I hadn't taken the ring, none of this was really my fault. But I *felt* responsible for everything: for the fact that we'd had to give up our Saturday afternoon for this meeting, and for the trouble that the club was headed for.

"I'm sorry, guys," I said quietly.

Dawn gave me a puzzled look.

"Oh, Stacey," said Kristy. "You have nothing to be sorry for. It's not *your* fault Mrs. Gardella is a wacko."

"She's not a wacko," I replied. "And I know it's not my fault. But still, I feel responsible."

"Why don't you tell us what's going on?"

Claud said impatiently to Kristy. She probably had some art project planned for the day, and now she was stuck at this meeting.

"You mean you didn't tell them yet?" I asked Kristy.

"Nope, I thought you should explain, from the beginning."

Oh, my lord.

I took a deep breath and started to talk. I told my friends the whole story. I told them about the way the Gardellas treated their pets, and about how dressed up they'd been, and about Tara's fancy room. I told them that the job had gone well, and that Mr. Gardella had paid me even more than I expected.

So far, so good. Everybody was interested, and I could see that nobody could guess what was coming next.

"So then," I went on, plunging ahead, "I get this phone call at the crack of dawn this morning. It was Mrs. Gardella!"

"What did she want?" asked Claud.

"She wanted to know why I'd stolen her diamond ring!" I blurted it out. I felt the tears starting again, but I held them back.

"WHAT?" asked everybody at once.

"But I *didn't* steal it," I said quickly. I felt

myself getting red. I was thinking again about that birthstone ring, and I figured everybody else was, too. "I don't know *what* happened to it, but I had nothing to do with the fact that it disappeared."

Suddenly everybody was talking at once, asking me questions, making comments about Mrs. Gardella, and speculating on what had happened to the ring. I heard Mallory say something about what a coincidence it was that it was the same kind of ring as the one I'd seen at the mall. But it was just a casual comment. I knew she didn't mean anything by it.

"Hold on, hold on," yelled Kristy over the noise. "Let's let Stacey finish her story."

So I told them about the phone call. I told them exactly what Mrs. Gardella had said about the missing ring, and exactly what *I'd* said. And what my mother had said. It didn't take long.

Finally I got to the worst part, the part that was hardest to tell.

"And then, she said that not only did she not want *me* to sit for her again, but that she wouldn't hire *anybody* from the club."

"So what?" said Claud. "Who wants to sit

for them, anyway?" Claudia's a great best friend. She's always so loyal. I gave her a grateful look.

But then I had to tell them the rest. "And she said she was going to call our other clients and tell them what had happened."

There was silence in the room. Everybody looked completely stunned.

"How awful," whispered Dawn. "Nothing like this has ever happened before. What about the club's reputation?"

Mary Anne elbowed her in the side. "Dawn!" she said. "Can't you see that Stacey feels bad enough already?" Good old Mary Anne. You can count on her to be sensitive about other people's feelings. But Dawn was right.

"Dawn's right," I said out loud. "It *is* awful. But I don't know what we can do about it."

"What if we call all our clients first, and explain what really happened?" asked Jessi, thoughtfully.

"That might just stir up more trouble," answered Kristy. "I mean, what if Mrs. Gardella doesn't end up calling everybody? Then we would have brought up the problem for nothing and confused our clients."

"Yeah," agreed Claud. "If you go out of

your way to insist that you're innocent, people are going to wonder if you're actually guilty." Claud knows about that sort of stuff because of all those Nancy Drew books she reads.

"What if we try to convince Mrs. Gardella not to make the calls?" asked Dawn. She looked at me hopefully.

"I don't think we can talk her out of it if her mind's made up," I answered. I felt miserable. "I mean, she thinks it's the right thing to do, and in a way, she's right. If I *had* stolen something, people should know about it."

"But you didn't," said Kristy. "Don't even talk that way. It's *not* the right thing for her to do — it's like she's assuming that you're guilty. You're supposed to be innocent until proven guilty, right?"

"Right," I answered. "Let's hope our other clients go along with that kind of thinking."

"You know," said Mary Anne. "I bet they will. After all, most of our clients have been hiring us for a long time. They know we're honest. They know we would never steal."

"I hope you're right, Mary Anne," said Kristy. "Because our good reputation is the only thing we've got going for us right now. There's not much we can do about Mrs. Gardella."

I spent the rest of Saturday and all day Sunday hoping the whole thing would blow over without affecting the club. On Monday, school dragged. I was eager to get to our meeting that afternoon.

Finally, it was 5:30. Kristy called the meeting to order, and then I collected the dues. We talked for a while about what we had done over the weekend. We talked about what had happened at school that day (nothing much, in case you're wondering). We even talked about the weather (clear and crisp — we agreed that it had been a very nice day). We talked about everything except Mrs. Gardella and the missing diamond ring. And the whole time we were talking, what we were *really* doing was waiting for the phone to ring.

But it didn't.

I stared at the silent phone, wondering if there could be any other explanation. But I couldn't come up with anything. I checked the clock. Five-forty. Usually by that time we would have gotten at least one or two calls.

Our conversation lagged. Nobody had anything left to say, it seemed. Then, suddenly, the phone rang. We all dived for it, but I got it. "Hello?" I said eagerly. "Baby-sitters Club."

"Oh, sorry," said a voice on the other end.

"I was trying to reach the sewage treatment plant. Wrong number, I guess."

Any other time, I would have told everyone else what the woman had said, and we would have giggled over it for the rest of the meeting. But that day I didn't feel very funny, so I just said, "Wrong number," and put the phone down.

"Hmmm," said Kristy.

"What do you mean by *that*?" I asked. I felt she was trying to tell me something. "Maybe you think I should quit the club. Is that what you think?"

"Stacey, are you nuts?" she exclaimed. "I don't want you to quit the club. And I don't blame you for anything. All I said was, 'Hmmm.' "

I guess I was feeling a little jumpy.

We sat quietly for a few more minutes. I could hear Claud's digital clock clicking the minutes away. Soon the meeting would be over. Finally, at 5:48 (I know the exact time, since I was watching the clock so closely), the phone rang again. This time I let somebody else answer it.

"Hello?" said Kristy. "Oh, hi, Mrs. Braddock." She listened for a moment. "I'm sure we can fit you in," she said, giving the rest of us a little smile. "I'll call you back in a couple of minutes." When she'd hung up, she told us that Mrs. Braddock needed a sitter for Haley and Matt.

"Did she sound — weird at all?" I asked. "Like she might have heard any rumors or anything?" We've been sitting for the Braddocks for a long time. I wondered what Mrs. Braddock would think if Mrs. Gardella called her.

"She didn't, really," said Kristy. "And I didn't want to ask. I wonder if she's heard anything. Maybe she has, but she doesn't believe it."

"Well, anyway," said Mary Anne, looking at the record book. "We can certainly fit her in. We do have a few jobs that we lined up last week, but basically we're wide open. You're available, Kristy, and so are Stacey, Jessi, and Dawn."

"I don't want the job," I said quickly. Somehow I didn't feel that I should take any jobs when there were so few of them. The others worked it out among themselves, and Kristy called Mrs. Braddock back.

After that, we only got one other phone call, from Mrs. Newton. She's another of our longtime clients. She didn't sound any different than usual either. At least, not according to Claud, who had answered the phone. Once that job was set up, it was six o'clock and time for the meeting to end.

Was it just coincidence that we'd had such a slow meeting? There was no way to know. We'd have to wait and see what happened next. I decided to keep my fingers crossed for at least the next few days.

CHAPTER 8

Tuesday

Oh, boy. WARNING! There's a new kid on the block. On Burnt Hill Road, that is. And this little terror might just be a challenger to the "walking disaster" title that Jackie Rodowsky now holds. His name's Joey Conklin, and all I can say is watch out. He's a cute kid, and I don't think he means to cause chaos, but.... Anyway, I wasn't even sitting for him! I was sitting for Jenny and Andrea, and everything was going fine, until Mr. Trouble showed up.

Mary Anne is usually pretty levelheaded when it comes to dealing with difficult kids, so when I started to read her notebook entry, I knew that this Joey must really be something.

But, as she said, her day started off well. She was sitting for the Prezziosos that afternoon. Jenny Prezzioso is four, and she can be kind of a b-r-a-t. She's used to getting her own way, and she can be very definite about what "her way" means. I think she's starting to grow out of her spoiled phase a little, though. Ever since Andrea arrived, Jenny's had to be the big sister.

We were all worried about how well Jenny would handle having a new baby sister. We thought we were in for the biggest case of sibling rivalry in the history of the world. But Jenny surprised us. She *adores* Andrea, loves to help take care of her, and is one of the sweetest, most gentle big sisters I've ever seen.

"Hello, Mary Anne," said Mrs. Prezzioso, answering the door. "I'm so glad you're a few minutes early. My meeting time got changed, and I've really got to rush if I'm going to make it."

"No problem," said Mary Anne. She's almost always early — all of us are. You never know when parents are going to need a little extra time to tell you something about the kids, or finish dressing, or give you instructions about where to call them in an emergency.

Mrs. Prezzioso was getting her jacket out of the closet. "Andrea's napping, but she should be up in a half hour or so. And Jenny's — "

"Hi, Mary Anne!" said Jenny, bounding into the room.

"There's Jenny now," said Mrs. Prezzioso. "Good-bye, honey." She kissed Jenny. "Be good for Mary Anne. I'll be back soon." She grabbed her car keys and ran out the door.

Jenny looked excited. She barely seemed to notice that her mother had left. "Guess what! It's almost my birthday," she said with a big smile.

"It is?" asked Mary Anne. As far as she remembered, Jenny's birthday was months away. But kids always seem to think that their birthdays are around the corner.

"Yup!" said Jenny. "And guess how old I'm going to be."

"Ummm . . . forty-five?" asked Mary Anne.

"No, silly!" shrieked Jenny, giggling. "I'm going to be thirteen."

"Now *you're* being silly," said Mary Anne. "*I'm* thirteen. You're four."

"I know I'm four now," said Jenny. "But on my birthday I'm going to be thirteen."

"Sorry, sweetie," said Mary Anne. "I think you might have to try being five, first."

Jenny frowned.

"Anyway," said Mary Anne, "I think your birthday is still pretty far away." She noticed that Jenny was frowning even harder, and decided to avoid a scene. "But how about if we have a pretend birthday party today?" she continued, quickly. "We'll dress up, and invite all your dolls — and Andrea, too, of course — and have pretend cake and pretend presents. Okay?"

Jenny was jumping up and down with excitement. "A birthday party! A birthday party!" she yelled.

"Shhh," Mary Anne said. "Let's try not to wake Andrea until the party's all ready. Now, let's find a couple of presents to wrap up." Jenny cruised around the living room and chose three of her favorite toys: a Barbie (the one she calls "Hospital Barbie" because she got it when Mrs. P. was at the hospital having Andrea), a ratty old clown doll she calls Mr. Bog, and her find-the-picture book.

While she was looking, Mary Anne had found last Sunday's comics and a roll of tape.

"Ready to wrap them?" she asked. They sat on the living room floor and Mary Anne helped Jenny wrap her "gifts." Jenny became intent on her job. She wrinkled her brow and stuck her tongue out of the corner of her mouth. It was pretty cute, according to Mary Anne. Finally Jenny was done. *Covered* with a million pieces of tape, but done.

Meanwhile, Mary Anne had cut a cake out of a piece of cardboard. "Want to draw the decorations and the candles?" she asked Jenny. Jenny jumped up to find her crayons.

"Okay," said Mary Anne. "It looks like we're ready for our party. What do you want to wear?" They trooped up to Jenny's room to look over the possibilities. Jenny has quite a wardrobe. Her mother has always liked to dress her up like a "little princess." She has tons of dresses, all dripping with lace and floppy bows and satin ribbons. She has party shoes in every color and style you can imagine. And she has fancy tights with ruffles on the seat and polka-dot decorations.

In other words, it's no problem finding something for Jenny to dress up in.

But Mary Anne had to stifle a giggle when she saw what Jenny had chosen to wear to her party. She'd rummaged around in her dresser until she found a faded pair of overalls and a pink-striped sweatshirt that was a little too small. Then she chose a pair of pink sneakers.

"Are you sure that's what you want to wear?" she asked Jenny, and Jenny nodded firmly. "Okay, then," said Mary Anne. "Time to wake up Andrea and get the other guests to the party."

Jenny stayed in her room, rounding up her favorite dolls and stuffed animals. Mary Anne went to Andrea's room and found her already awake. She wasn't crying, or even looking unhappy. She was just relaxing in her crib, looking around the room with a big smile on her face.

"You look like you're ready for a party," said Mary Anne, picking her up. "As soon as I put a dry diaper on you, that is," she added, wrinkling her nose. Mary Anne laid Andrea on the changing table, and immediately Andrea broke into a loud wail. Jenny came running.

"Don't cry, Andrea!" she exclaimed. "We're going to have a birthday party, and you're invited." Andrea continued to cry. "Wait a minute," said Jenny. She ran out of the room. Two seconds later, she popped back in. This time she was holding a stuffed monkey. "Here, Andrea. Here's Monkey Matthew," she said. "Now do you feel better?"

Andrea's wails grew louder. Mary Anne struggled with the diaper's plastic tapes, trying to unfasten them. As Mary Anne worked at changing Andrea, Jenny kept running back and forth, bringing toys that she thought would cheer up her sister. It was a nice thing for a big sister to do, said Mary Anne later, but unfortunately, none of the toys did the trick.

Andrea finally stopped crying when Mary Anne finished with her diaper. Then Jenny helped pick out an outfit for her to wear to the party. Andrea's outfit was a little fancier than Jenny's. Jenny chose a pink nightgown with lacy trim, and a "princess" crown from the dress-up box.

"She looks so beautiful," said Jenny. "Maybe it should be *Andrea's* birthday that we're having the party for."

"Great idea," said Mary Anne. They headed downstairs and into the kitchen. Mary Anne poured juice for Jenny to have with her pretend cake. Andrea got a bottle. Jenny sang "Happy Birthday" five times for her sister, becoming louder and more off-key with each version.

Then Jenny "helped" Andrea open her presents. Even though she'd wrapped them only minutes ago, Jenny shrieked with surprise as each present was opened.

"These presents are only pretend, though," she reminded Andrea seriously. "You can play with them for today, but they're really still *my* toys."

Andrea smiled and said, "Glug."

"You're welcome," said Jenny. "Now can we play outside?" she asked, turning to Mary Anne.

Mary Anne nodded. "As soon as we clean up from our party," she said, picking up the "wrapping paper" and putting the "cake" aside.

It was a beautiful day outside, and Mary Anne relaxed on the porch with Andrea while Jenny performed "ballet" on the front lawn. Then Mary Anne saw a little boy peeking through the bushes at the edge of the lawn. He was watching Jenny, and it was obvious that he wanted to play. He seemed a little shy, though. "Hi!" Mary Anne called. "What's your name?"

"That's Joey, silly!" yelled Jenny. "Hi, Joey! Want to play tag?"

Soon Jenny and Joey were running happily around the yard, shrieking with laughter as they fought over who was "It." Andrea sat happily in Mary Anne's lap, watching them play.

Then she grew restless. She squirmed and wiggled and kicked. "Okay, Andrea," said Mary Anne. "I get the message. You're bored." She stood up, holding Andrea, and walked around the yard, singing softly to her.

She walked up and down the side yard until Andrea's eyes began to close. "Ready for another nap?" she said. "Okay, let's go inside." Mary Anne looked for Jenny and Joey, planning to invite them inside, too, but they were nowhere to be seen. Mary Anne's heart began to pound. How could she have lost two kids? She'd been looking right at them just a couple of minutes ago.

"Jenny!" she called. "Joey!" She walked around to the front door — until she saw something that made her hurry. It was a hose, the garden hose that was usually coiled up behind some shrubbery next to the porch. Only now, it ran from the outside faucet, over the lawn, through the shrubs, onto the porch, and through the front door!

That hose couldn't be on, Mary Anne said to herself as she ran, holding Andrea carefully. It just couldn't. She threw open the front door and stopped short. There was Jenny, laughing wildly. There was Joey, holding the hose. And there was water — all over *everything.* Joey was watering the front hall and its furniture.

Mary Anne was stunned. For a moment she didn't even know what to say. Then she did. "Joey!" she said loudly. "Get that hose out of the house. Now!" She rushed over to him and guided him out the door. "Now turn off the faucet," she added, watching him from the porch. Joey ran to the faucet.

"And now," she said, "I think it's time for you to go home." Joey looked at her with big eyes. So far, he hadn't said a word. He turned to leave the yard. "Wait a minute, Joey," called Mary Anne. "What's your last name? I want to call your mommy."

"Umm," said Joey. He looked around, pretending not to know it.

"Conklin!" said Jenny from behind Mary Anne. "His last name is Conklin."

"Thank you, Jenny," Mary Anne replied. "Good-bye, Joey Conklin." She walked back into the front hall, still carrying Andrea. "Oh, boy," she said, looking at all the water. "Oh, boy."

She spent most of the rest of the day undoing what Joey had done. First, she put Andrea down for a nap, since Andrea had been getting sleepy anyway. Then she called Mrs. Conklin. Then she settled Jenny with some crayons and paper. Then she got out the mop. It was a long afternoon.

"No, I don't think there was any permanent damage," said Mary Anne. "Except maybe to my nerves. Can you imagine? Watch out for that Joey."

The members of the BSC had been talking about Mary Anne's experience at the Prezziosos'. It was 5:35 on Wednesday, and Kristy had called our meeting to order. Nobody had brought up the situation with the Gardellas, and I was glad. I'd been thinking about it for days, and I needed a break.

Claudia, Dawn, and Mary Anne were sprawled on Claud's bed, munching on Smartfood. Kristy was perched in the director's chair, as usual. I was sitting on the floor that day, with my back against the bed, facing Jessi and Mal. They were looking through a book of Claud's called *The Horse in Art*.

"Why do you think they call it Smartfood,

anyway?" asked Claud. "I mean, how can popcorn make you smart?" She threw a handful into her mouth. "Even if it is incredibly delicious."

"I don't think they mean it makes you smart," said Mary Anne. "I think they mean that you're smart if you buy it. Because it's kind of a healthy snack — I mean, compared to Ring-Dings or something."

"Let me try some," said Mal. "If there's any chance that it does make you smart, I should eat a whole bunch. I have a math test tomorrow and I don't think I'm going to understand any of the *questions*, much less come up with the right answers."

At that moment I realized something was wrong. Ordinarily, Kristy would not put up with "non-club" conversation going on for so long. She makes us concentrate on club business between 5:30 and 6:00. But that day she didn't seem to be paying atttention to the chatter that was going on. She was just staring at the phone with this fierce expression on her face, as if she could make it ring.

But it sat there silently.

I started to worry. I didn't think I could stand it if I had to sit through another meeting where nobody (or hardly anybody) called. I began to stare at the phone, too. And after a little more conversation about the good points and bad points of various kinds of junk food (Claud's favorite topic), everybody else shut up, too. So there we were, all seven of us, sitting in Claud's room and staring at a quiet phone.

Then it rang.

"All right!" yelled Kristy. She composed herself quickly and picked up the phone. "Baby-sitters Club," she said. We watched her carefully as she spoke to the person on the other end. It's always fun to try to guess who the caller is, just by listening to one end of the conversation.

"Sure, Mrs. Sobak," Kristy said after a while. "I understand. Wednesday at 4:30. That's fine."

Well, we didn't have to guess anymore. Mrs. Sobak must have been calling for a sitter for Betsy, her eight-year-old daughter. As Kristy hung up, Mary Anne pulled out the record book, a puzzled expression on her face. "Didn't we already — " she began to ask.

"Yup," said Kristy. "We *did* already arrange that job. I was supposed to take it. But Mrs. Sobak wasn't calling to hire us. She was calling to cancel."

Everybody gasped. "Cancel?" asked Dawn. "Why?"

I squeezed my eyes shut, wishing that I could cover my ears, too. I didn't want to hear what I thought Kristy was going to say, that Mrs. Sobak had talked to Mrs. Gardella and didn't want to use our club anymore.

"Betsy's uncle is coming to town," said Kristy. "And Mrs. Sobak wants Betsy to have a chance to visit with him. He's going to take her to the zoo that afternoon."

I let out a breath. "Really?" I asked. What a relief.

"Well, that's what she said," answered Kristy. She sounded a bit doubtful. "Who knows if that's the *real* reason?"

My stomach flip-flopped. I felt *so* guilty, even though this wasn't really my fault.

"Do you think the real reason could be that Mrs. Gar — " began Mal, but Jessi elbowed her in the ribs.

"Shhh," she said. "Don't even say it."

Everybody was quiet again after that. And the phone was quiet, too. I was beginning to feel sick to my stomach. Our meetings are usually so much fun, but this one was a disaster.

"This is the worst," said Dawn suddenly. "What are we going to do?"

"I don't know," said Kristy. "But you know what? I was thinking last night that this club has been through some pretty bad times before, and we've always managed to come out on top. I'm sure we'll work out this problem, too."

She sounded pretty certain. I wasn't so confident.

"What's the worst thing that's ever happened to the club?" asked Jessi. She looked interested. "I mean, if you don't mind talking about it."

We thought for a minute.

"It was when — " began Mary Anne.

"It must have been — " said Dawn at the same time.

"You go ahead," said Mary Anne.

"No, you," said Dawn. "You've been in the club longer."

"Well," said Mary Anne. "I was going to say that the worst time *I* remember was when we had that humongous fight and none of us was speaking to the others. Remember?"

Kristy, Claudia, and I all nodded. "Boy, do I remember. Believe it or not," I said to Jessi, "we were all so mad at each other that we couldn't even stand to be in the same room. So instead of having meetings — "

"We each took turns sitting here alone answering the phone!" finished Kristy. "Oh, that was so ridiculous."

"What was the fight *about*?" asked Mallory.

"Well, that's the funny part," said Kristy. "I was thinking about it last night, and I couldn't even remember."

"I remember," said Dawn quietly. "I wasn't in the club yet, but that fight happened right before I joined. In fact, Mary Anne and I met because she had nobody to sit with at lunch! I was new in town, so we were both feeling lonely. Of course, I didn't know at first that she *did* actually have friends, but that she wasn't speaking to any of them at the time."

"So what was the fight about?" asked Jessi.

"Well," said Dawn, "it had to do with the way we sometimes used to take jobs without checking first to see who was available."

"Job-hogging!" yelled Claudia. "Now I remember. And Mary Anne told us all off. Can you believe it?"

"That's right," said Kristy. "Job-hogging. But then we kept getting madder and madder at each other for all kinds of other reasons, and by the time we were finally ready to make up, we couldn't even be sure who needed to apologize to whom for what."

"So we had a group apology," I said. "Want to show them what we did?" I asked the others. "Ready? One, two, three — "

"I'm sorry!" Claud, Kristy, Mary Anne, and I chorused at once. Then we cracked up. We were laughing so hard that we almost didn't hear the phone ring. Jessi grabbed it.

"Hello?" she said. "Oh, hello, Mrs. Addison, how are you?" She paused for a moment. "I'm sorry to hear that," she went on, looking glum. "I hope you both feel better soon. Thanks for calling." She hung up and looked around the room.

"You're not going to believe this," she said. "Mrs. Addison just cancelled, too."

"You're kidding!" said Claud. "That was *my* job. On Saturday night, right?"

"Right," answered Jessi. "She and her husband were supposed to go to the theater. But now she and Corrie have strep throat, and the doctor said she should avoid being in public, since strep is so contagious."

"Oh, no!" said Claud. "I really needed that job, too. I'm broke." She looked depressed.

"Hey Kristy, tell us about another rough

time," said Mallory. I think she was trying to change the subject and get our minds off what was happening.

"Well," began Kristy, thinking.

"I know," I said. "What about the time those girls started the Baby-sitters Agency and tried to steal our clients?"

"Oh, my lord," said Claud. "That was really the worst. Remember, Kristy? You wanted us to try to compete with them by lowering our prices and offering house-cleaning services for no extra charge."

"What?" said Jessi and Mal at the same time.

"Don't worry," said Kristy. "They talked me out of it. And the Agency self-destructed because the sitters they hired were so terrible."

"But you know what?" said Claud. "I just remembered. They *did* steal some of our clients — for a while. And during that time, we'd have meetings when the phone never rang. Just like now."

"You're right," said Mary Anne. "And we survived that, didn't we?" She sounded optimistic. But then she looked down at the record book. "I have to say, though, that things don't look so good. We hardly have any jobs lined up for the next week. And the ones we *do* have are mostly for the Pikes and the Ramseys and the Brewers."

Were we reduced to sitting only for our families? This didn't look good. But we spent the last few minutes of the meeting talking about other bad times the club had been through, and by the end of it I felt a little better. The phone hadn't rung again, but at least I had the feeling that things might work out. I had no idea *how,* but I was hoping for the best.

Thursday

I never thought that sitting for my own brother and sister could be so exciting. Exciting? Well, maybe *terrifying* is the word I'm looking for. Luckily, Becca and Squirt never had any idea how truly frightened I was. And I'm kind of proud of myself for managing to hide my fear.

Jessi was sitting for Becca and Squirt on Thursday night. Her parents had gone to a dinner party, and her Aunt Cecelia, who lives with them, had gone to the movies. Jessi says she always has a good time sitting for Becca and Squirt, but she doesn't get to do it as often, since Aunt Cecelia came to live with the Ramseys. Jessi's aunt would probably prefer to be the full-time sitter for the Ramseys, since she thinks she's the only one who knows the right way to do things. But once in a while, Jessi lucks out and Aunt Cecelia has plans on the same night Mr. and Mrs. Ramsey do.

"Hey, Squirt," said Jessi. "Let me see your ba." "Ba" is what Squirt calls his belly button, and he loves pulling up his shirt to show it off. You should see his grin when he does it. He looks so, so proud of himself. It's a riot.

They were sitting around in the living room after dinner (Jessi had made hot dogs and beans, Becca's favorite), listening to the radio, and trying to decide what to do next. Becca wanted to play Clue, but Jessi vetoed that idea.

"We have to play something we can play together," she said. "Squirt can't play Clue."

"Squirt can't play *anything*," said Becca. "He's just a baby."

"Well, maybe he can't play any board games, but if we think, I'm sure we can come up with some kind of game Squirt can play." Jessi and Becca sat quietly for a few minutes, thinking. Squirt continued to show off his ba, even though nobody was paying attention.

"I know," said Jessi. She picked up a button that had been lying on the table. It had fallen off her father's shirt just as her parents were getting ready to leave.

"Let's play a new kind of hide-and-seek. I'll hide this button somewhere in the room, and then you try to find it. Squirt loves to look for things, so he'll have a good time."

"What happens when I find it?" asked Becca. She didn't sound convinced that the game would be fun.

"Then you get to hide it and I'll look," answered Jessi.

"Okay," said Becca. "Let's try it. I'll close my eyes while you hide the button." She squinched up her eyes and held Squirt on her lap. "Close your eyes, Squirt," she said. "Like me." Squirt squinched up his eyes, too.

Jessi looked around the room. The Ramseys' living room isn't all that big, but there are plenty of places where you could hide something as little as a button. She didn't want to make the game too hard, though, because then Becca would get frustrated.

Finally, she put it underneath one of the magazines stacked on the coffee table. "Ready!" she said, as soon as she'd made sure the magazines were back in their original positions.

Becca opened her eyes and started to roam around the room. Squirt followed her, picking up everything that she picked up, looking into every corner that she looked into, poking his fingers between the sofa cushions the same way she did. He was having a ball.

Jessi watched as Becca narrowed down the hiding places. But every time Becca approached the coffee table, she'd get distracted by another idea and look somewhere else. Jessi wanted to giggle, but she controlled herself. She knew the game wasn't easy. She waited patiently, singing along to the song that was on the radio.

Finally, Becca went to the coffee table and started to pick up each magazine in turn. "I found it!" she squealed, when she turned over the one that was hiding the button. "I found it, Squirt."

Squirt squealed, too. He was almost as happy as Becca was.

"Okay," said Jessi. "Now, let's go to another room and *you* get to hide the button." They trooped into the kitchen. "Hey," said Jessi, when they got there, "I know. Instead of hiding a button in this room, let's hide this." She held up a little bottle opener. "We'll use a different object in each room."

"Close your eyes!" commanded Becca, and Jessi closed her eyes. She heard the refrigerator door open and shut, and then the sound of cabinet doors closing. She heard the rustle of paper bags. Then it was quiet. "Okay," said Becca.

Jessi and Squirt began to search the kitchen. They looked in every corner, and under every appliance. They looked in the sink, and they even checked the oven. Jessi opened the refrigerator and peered inside. No bottle opener. Finally, she opened the silverware drawer. There was the opener, where it was usually kept!

Becca giggled. "Good trick, right?" she asked.

"Good trick," agreed Jessi. "You know, I think it took me a lot longer to find that than it took you to find the button. We should time our searches so we know who's faster. That would really make the game good." She dug around in a drawer and found the egg timer. "This will work," she said. "Let's go into the dining room."

They played for quite a while. Jessi hid Squirt's favorite toy — a blue plastic fish — in the dining room, and then Becca hid a toothbrush in the bathroom. Jessi hid one of her ballet shoes in her bedroom, and then Becca hid her Barbie in *her* bedroom. Squirt trailed along everywhere they went, giggling happily whenever an object was found. *He* never found anything, but he didn't seem to care.

The girls timed their searches to see who was faster, and Becca kept winning. "You're good at this game, Becca," said Jessi.

"I like to look for things," replied Becca. "This is fun."

Then they went into their parents' room. It was Jessi's turn to hide something, and she chose one of her mother's earrings from her dressing table. While Becca closed her eyes, Jessi looked for a good place. An earring was so small she could put it almost anywhere.

"Hey, wait a minute," she said out loud.

Becca opened her eyes. "What?" she asked.

"I'm just thinking . . . " said Jessi. "Never mind. Close your eyes again." She hid the earring under a pillow and then watched while Becca searched. And as she watched, she thought. While she had been looking for a place, she'd suddenly realized how many hiding places there could be in a house. And then she thought of Mrs. Gardella's ring. She'd known all along that I hadn't stolen it, but now she had some ideas about what might have happened to it. It could easily have been misplaced. It could be anywhere!

As soon as Becca found the earring, Jessi hurried her sister and brother downstairs. She was planning to call me and tell me what she'd been thinking. Maybe the Gardellas simply hadn't looked hard enough. Becca and Squirt ran into the kitchen to find a snack. Jessi followed them. But as she walked through the living room, she was stopped in her tracks by something she heard on the radio. It was a news flash, and since she was listening to WSTO — the Voice of Stoneybrook — she knew it must be local news. The word that had made her stop and listen was "thief."

"A professional and possibly dangerous thief is still at large in the area," said the announcer. "Police report that he has broken into several homes in the past two weeks, and they've had calls reporting three burglaries tonight alone. Homeowners are warned to lock their doors and windows, hide their valuables, and take other precautions. Anyone who has information on the matter should call the police at — "

Jessi snapped off the radio. She glanced around. She could hear her brother and sister laughing in the kitchen. Whew. At least Becca hadn't heard about the thief.

But Jessi was terrified. There was a burglar on the loose in Stoneybrook, and he could be looking into the living room window at that very moment! Uh-oh, she thought. What am I going to do now?

Her first thought, she told me later, was to call her parents. She knew they'd come straight home, and then everything would be okay. No burglar was going to rob a home that was full of people, and anyway, she'd feel safer if her parents were there. But she threw away that thought in a second. If she called her parents, she would prove to Aunt Cecelia (who would be sure to hear about it later) that Jessi wasn't "mature" enough to sit for Becca and Squirt. Then she'd *never* get to sit for them.

Jessi pulled herself together. The thing to do, she realized, would be to make the house as secure as possible — but without letting

Becca and Squirt know what she was doing. She began by checking to see that all the windows were locked. She tried the living room windows, and then went into the kitchen and checked those.

"What are you doing, Jessi?" asked Becca.

"Oh, well . . . " said Jessi, thinking fast. "It just seems like it might be getting a little chilly outside, and I wanted to be sure the windows were closed tight."

"Can I help?" asked Becca.

"Sure," said Jessi, and she and Becca (with Squirt following along) walked through the house checking windows. Jessi also checked the doors, when Becca wasn't looking.

"We should be pretty warm now," said Becca, after they'd checked the last window.

"Right," said Jessi. "But . . . doesn't it seem kind of dark and gloomy in here? Let's turn on some more lights." She figured the burglar wouldn't want to break into a house that was all lit up, so she went from room to room, turning on every light. Her father would kill her when the electric bill came, but she figured it was worth it.

"Let's help Mama clean up," she said, when they had reached her parents' bedroom. She swept her mother's jewelry off the top of her dressing table and into a drawer. After all, the newscaster had said to "hide valuables." What other valuables did they have?

She thought for a minute. "You know," she said to Becca, who was beginning to look at her with a puzzled expression, "since we're not watching the TV, maybe we should cover it up. It'll look neater. The VCR, too."

Jessi threw a blanket over the TV and VCR. "Now," she said. "Let's have some music." She flicked on the radio and found a station playing rock music. Then she turned up the volume as loud as it would go. She wanted to make absolutely sure the thief would know that someone was home.

"Let's dance!" exclaimed Jessi. She grabbed Squirt, swung him up, and danced him around the living room. Becca gave her a funny look, but then her favorite song came on and she shrugged and started dancing, too.

In the middle of the song, Jessi had an awful thought. Could the *thief* have stolen Mrs. Gardella's ring? Could he have been in the house while Stacey was baby-sitting? "Oh, my lord," she said out loud — but nobody heard her because the music was so loud. That was the scariest thing Jessi could imagine.

When Mrs. and Mr. Ramsey came home,

they found Jessi reading on the couch, with the radio on — loudly. Becca and Squirt had managed to fall asleep, but every light in the house was on, including the ones in their rooms.

Jessi explained the situation to her parents, and they told her they were proud of her. Then she went to bed. Now that they were home, she felt safe as she drifted off to sleep. And her last thought before she slept made her smile. If the thief *had* taken the ring, she thought, then Stacey's name would be cleared. And the Baby-sitters Club would be back to normal business.

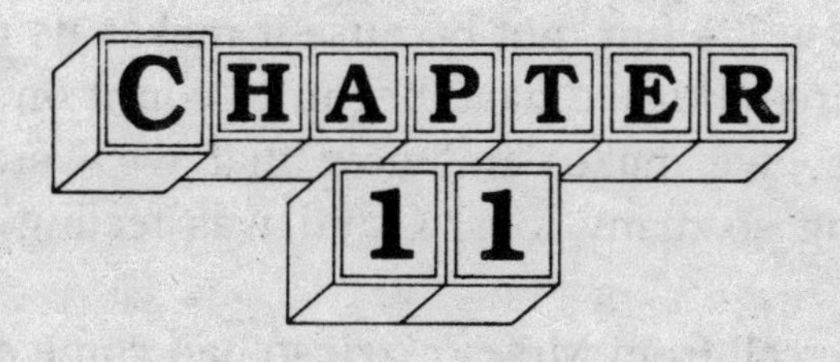

Saturday

I reely do apresh apprish apreciate — Im realy greatful to you guys for leting me have the job at the Pretziosa's, sinse my other job at the Adison's got canseled. I relly do need the money these days. Even if it meens sitting for Genny, who can be such a pane. (You were rite, though, Mary Anne — she has goten better latley.) But I wuld have liked to stay their for more than just an hour and a half. I was counting on being paid for at leest three. Now Im going to have to return those pink sneekers. If I want to by any art supplies this month, that is.

Claud isn't usually so obsessed with how much money she makes. Most of us baby-sit because it's fun, not because it makes us millionaires. But we have begun to count on the money we make, and now that we weren't getting so many jobs, Claud was feeling the pinch.

The call from Mrs. Prezzioso had come during Friday's meeting. It was one of the only calls we'd gotten.

"I wonder," Kristy had said after she'd hung up. "Do you think the Prezziosos just haven't heard the Gardella story?"

"Maybe they have but they're desperate for a sitter," Dawn had said. "Anyway, who gets the job?"

Mary Anne checked the record book. "Well, the only ones free are Claud, Kristy, Mal, and Stacey."

I didn't want the job, because I still felt guilty about what had happened. And Kristy and Mal had said they were still getting jobs sitting for their brothers and sisters, so they didn't need the money as much as Claud did. Claud had accepted the job gratefully.

So there she was that Saturday night, saying good-bye to Mr. and Mrs. Prezzioso as they headed out for a party. They were all dressed up and Mrs. P. was "reeking of perfume," as Claud said later. They really seemed to be looking forward to their night out.

"Okay, Jenny," said Claud, after they'd left. "Let's get your little sister ready for bed."

"Can I pick out her pajamas?" asked Jenny.

"Sure," Claud answered. She led the way to Andrea's room. "Which ones do you want her to wear?"

Jenny picked out a pair of blue pajamas with pink dinosaurs on them. "These are her favorite ones," she said. She helped Claud diaper Andrea and then put on the pajamas. ("Helping" meant mostly just standing around and saying, "Mommy doesn't do it like that," and other useful things.)

Then they went back downstairs to get a bottle for Andrea. Mrs. Prezzioso had left one in the bottle warmer, so it was all ready. They trooped back to Andrea's room. Claud sat in the rocker with the baby, hoping that the motion would help her to fall asleep once she'd finished her bottle.

Jenny ran into her own room and found her favorite doll, then dragged her little children's-sized rocker into Andrea's room and set it next to the big rocker. "I'm going to put *my* baby to bed, too," she said. She tipped a doll's bottle toward her "baby's" mouth, and held the doll while she rocked slowly.

Claud started to sing softly to Andrea. " 'Hush, little baby, don't say a word.' "

Jenny sang to her baby, too. " 'Twinkle, twinkle, little star.' " It wasn't exactly a lullaby, but it was a song she knew.

Claudia and Jenny rocked next to each other until Claud noticed that Andrea's eyes were drooping. "Oh, you're getting sleepy, aren't you?" she said. She put down the bottle and lifted Andrea to her shoulder, patting her on the back.

Jenny burped her baby, too.

Then Claud gently lowered Andrea into her crib. "Go to sleep now," she said, rubbing Andrea's back softly.

Jenny put her doll on the floor in a little nest she'd made of blankets. "Time to sleep," she said, rubbing the doll's back.

Then Claud and Jenny tiptoed out of the room. "You're a good mommy," said Claud.

"I know," said Jenny. "I watch what *my* mommy does and I do the same things."

"What's your baby's name?" asked Claud. She was expecting maybe Ashley or Melissa.

"Pee-wee," answered Jenny seriously.

Claud had to stifle a giggle.

"He's my favorite on TV, so I named my baby after him," explained Jenny.

Claud kept a straight face and nodded. "Well, Pee-wee is a very good baby," she said. "Now, what would you like to do until bedtime?"

"Let's play house," said Jenny. "You be the mommy and I'll be the little baby." She crouched on the floor and started to crawl around.

Claudia smiled. She knows that older brothers and sisters sometimes like to play "baby" so they can get the same kind of attention their siblings are getting. "Does the baby want a bottle?" she asked.

"Waaa!" answered Jenny. "Baby want a bottle."

Claudia went into the kitchen and put some apple juice into an empty bottle. "Here you go," she said, bringing it to Jenny. Jenny crawled into Claud's lap and started drinking out of the bottle. Then she wiggled out again. "Waaa!" she said. "Baby want toys."

Claud pulled out a few of Andrea's baby toys out of the toy basket. "Here you go, baby," she said, giving them to Jenny. Jenny took them and started to throw them around the living room, looking at Claud out of the corner of her eye.

"No, no, little baby," said Claud. "Baby shouldn't throw toys."

"Waaa!" cried Jenny. Then, as quickly as she'd become a baby, she became a little girl again. "I'm tired of this game," she said. "Let's play Shark Attack."

So Claud played Shark Attack with Jenny until the shark's batteries wore down and he stopped moving around the board. Then she and Jenny played with Barbie dolls for a while. They had finished with that and were about to start on a game of hide-and-seek when Claud looked at her watch.

"Oops!" she said. "It's eight-fifteen, and you're supposed to be in bed by eight-thirty. Time to brush your teeth and get ready for bed." As they marched up the stairs together, Claud was already thinking about what she'd do after Jenny was asleep. She knew the Prezziosos wouldn't be home until at least ten-thirty, so she figured she'd have time to finish her math homework. For once she'd remembered to bring her school stuff with her.

Just as she was squeezing the toothpaste onto Jenny's brush, Claud heard a funny noise downstairs. She tensed up. Jessi had told us about the report she'd heard on the radio, and I think we were all a little nervous about burglars. Claud's an experienced enough sitter to be able to control her fears, though, so she hadn't thought much about thieves that night. And of course she'd made sure the doors were locked after the Prezziosos left.

But now she stopped what she was doing and listened closely. The noise had stopped. She handed Jenny's toothbrush to her, then stood by the bathroom door to listen some more. She heard the noise again! It sounded exactly like the door opening downstairs. "Oh, my lord," Claudia muttered.

"Whzzt?" asked Jenny, her mouth full of toothpaste.

"Nothing," said Claud. "Keep on brushing. You're doing a good job." As soon as Jenny turned back to the mirror, Claudia tiptoed into the hall.

"Claudia?" someone called from downstairs.

Claudia told me later that she nearly jumped through the ceiling. But she pulled herself together fast. "Mrs. Prezzioso!" she said. "What are you doing home so early?"

Mr. and Mrs. Prezzioso were climbing the stairs together. "Why don't you put Jenny to bed," Mrs. P. said to her husband. "I'll talk to Claudia." She led Claudia into the bedroom and motioned for her to sit on the bed. "Don't worry. Everything's all right," said Mrs. P. She must have noticed the look on Claud's face.

"What happened?" asked Claudia.

"Well, we were at this dinner party," said Mrs. P., "and another couple, the Gardellas, were there, too."

Claud drew in a breath. "I can ex — " she started.

"It's okay," said Mrs. P. "We didn't believe what they were telling us. We've hired you girls as sitters for so long that we think we know you pretty well. And we know that none of you would ever steal from a client."

Claudia let out the breath she'd taken. "But why did you come home?" she asked.

"Well, we were kind of upset by what the Gardellas were saying. It turned the evening sour for us. I didn't want to have an argument with them, so we just left," said Mrs. P.

Claud was impressed. "Wow," she said. "You really believe in us."

"Of course I do," said Mrs. P. "Besides," she added in a lower voice, "between you and me, the party was a real dud. I didn't mind leaving."

Claud laughed. "Thanks for your support," she said. "But even if the party was no fun, I'm sorry you had to leave. You were looking forward to your night out."

"I know," said Mrs. P. "But we'll go out again soon." She rummaged in her purse. "Here's pay for two hours' work," she said. "I'm sorry I can't pay you for the whole time."

Claud was sorry, too. She'd been counting on that money. But, as she told me later, what could she say? Mrs. P. was being so nice. She left their house feeling pretty good, but by the time Mr. P. had driven her home, Claudia had had more time to think and she was fuming. How could the Gardellas *do* that? How could they spread rumors about the club? It just wasn't fair.

On that same Saturday night, while Claud was sitting, I was home with my mom. In a way I was glad I didn't have a sitting job that night. Ever since Mom started working again, I don't get to spend too much time with her, and I kind of miss her. We've gotten pretty close since the divorce (even though we still fight occasionally, as you know), and I honestly like just hanging out with her.

We'd made dinner together, after deciding that we both felt like spaghetti. I threw together a salad while she made a quick tomato sauce. Then we brought all the stuff to the table. It looked great, and I was starving. I helped myself to a big plate of spaghetti and sprinkled cheese all over it.

"So, no sitting job tonight?" asked my mom.

"No, no sitting job tonight, or tomorrow night, or any other night this week," I answered glumly. Suddenly my spaghetti didn't look so good.

"Oh, Stacey," said my mom. "I'm sorry. Listen, I'm sure it's just a coincidence that business is slow. Your club has so many loyal clients. I know they wouldn't desert you."

"You're probably right," I said. But I'm sure I didn't sound too convinced — because I wasn't. Mom changed the subject, trying to distract me. She talked about the weather. She discussed the news of the day. She explained why she had decided to stop buying white bread. She told me about her job. But if she'd given me a pop quiz the next day on everything she said, I'm sorry to say I would have failed it. I just wasn't listening too well. I know that isn't nice, but I couldn't help it. My mind was on other things.

After dinner, I cleared the table and washed the dishes, without even being asked. After all, I figured, I had nothing better to do. I was almost finished when my mom walked into the kitchen. I must have looked pretty depressed, because she gave me a big hug.

"Come on, honey, cheer up!" she said. "Listen, how about if we rent a movie and watch it together?"

"Okay," I said. "Why not?"

We drove to the video store and spent what seemed like *hours* picking out something. Everything I wanted to see she had no interest in, and vice versa. "How about this?" I asked, holding up a horror movie about some girls at summer camp. I'd heard it was really good.

"Ugh!" said Mom. "I don't know how you can watch that junk. Now this," she said, holding up another movie box, "is a *real* movie. *Holiday,* starring Cary Grant and Katharine Hepburn. Oh, is Cary Grant handsome! Don't you think?" She showed me the picture.

"He's cute, I guess," I said, although I couldn't really see what was so great about him. "But don't tell me that movie's in black and white. No way!"

She put the box back. We both kept looking. "How about this?" I asked. I'd found a concert film featuring my favorite group.

Mom shook her head. "I don't even like their records. I don't think I could stand watching them for two hours." She held up the box she'd been looking at. "This one is a classic."

"*It's a Wonderful Life*?" I said. "I can't say I agree with *that* these days. And anyway, I just don't feel like watching a 'classic.' "

But then I found a classic I love — a movie

I could watch over and over again. And it's even in color. "What do you say, Mom?" I asked, holding up the box. She gave me the thumbs-up-sign, so I brought the box to the counter. *Gone With the Wind*. I think we've seen it about ten times, but we still love it. It's one movie we can always agree to watch together.

We drove home, and while Mom went into the kitchen to make popcorn, I went upstairs to check my blood sugar and give myself some insulin.

Then we settled in to watch the movie. By then I was feeling better about things. The popcorn was great, and as soon as I heard that *Gone With the Wind* theme music I was in heaven. But ten minutes into the movie, the phone rang. "I'll get it," I said.

"Should I stop the VCR?" Mom asked.

"Just for a minute," I answered, as I picked up the phone. "Hello?" I said.

It was Claudia, and she sounded upset. Quickly, she told me what had happened at the Prezziosos. "This has really gotten out of hand," she said. "It's one thing when we don't get a lot of jobs, but then when I finally *do* get a job, it ends after an hour and a half!"

I felt terrible. "Maybe business will pick up again next week," I said hopefully.

"Not if the Gardellas have their way, it won't," she said. "Listen, how about if I come over? It's still early. I'm sure my dad won't mind driving me there."

"Sure," I replied, "I'd love to see my best friend." We always turn to each other in bad times. After I'd hung up, I asked my mom if she wouldn't mind watching the movie by herself, since Claudia was coming over. I figured Claud and I would just hang out in my room. Maybe talking about the situation would make her feel better.

Mom understood. "Sounds like Claudia needs a friend right now," she said. "I'll be fine with Rhett and Scarlett for company."

But when Claud arrived and we went upstairs, she didn't seem to want any comforting. In fact, she seemed kind of cool toward me, and she wasn't talking much.

"So tell me again," I said. "Exactly what did Mrs. Prezzioso say when she came home?"

Claudia was roaming around my room, picking things up and putting them down. She didn't look at me when she answered my question. "She said Mrs. Gardella seemed convinced that you had taken her ring, but that Mrs. P. didn't believe her."

"Well, that's good," I said. "I mean, Mrs. P. knows me pretty well. And anybody who knows me knows I wouldn't steal."

"Yeah, well . . . " Claud drifted over to my dressing table.

"So did she say anything else?" I asked.

"Just that the party was ruined for her and she didn't want to stay." Now Claud was looking through my makeup, moving around my bottles and brushes and compacts.

"Do you want to try some of that new blush I got?" I asked. "It's really a good color for me. I wonder whether it would work on you, too."

"What? Oh, no," said Claud. She seemed distracted, as if she were somewhere else.

"Claud," I said. "What's the matter?"

"Nothing's the matter," she answered. "Nothing at all." But she sounded kind of mad. I was beginning to feel that something weird was happening between us.

I tried to ignore it. "So what did Mrs. P. wear to the party?" I asked. "She always looks like she stepped out of a magazine."

"I don't really remember," replied Claud.

Something was *definitely* up. Claud always pays a lot of attention to clothes. She can remember every outfit she's worn to school over a whole season, and she tries never to repeat the exact same outfit.

I looked closely at what Claudia was doing. She had finished checking out my makeup, and had started to look through my jewelry. I heard the tinkle of my musical jewelry box as she opened its lid. Then I watched as she started to look through my things. I couldn't figure out what she was up to. She's seen my stuff a million times before. In fact, she's borrowed most of it once or twice. We're always trading jewelry back and forth. But Claud looked serious this time as she checked each one of the little drawers and pulled out necklaces, earrings, and rings.

Rings.

All of a sudden I realized what she was doing. She was looking for Mrs. Gardella's diamond ring! Even *Claudia*, my best friend, had become suspicious of me. I couldn't believe it.

"Claud, I know what you're doing," I said. My stomach was in a knot. "You're looking for that ring, aren't you?"

Claudia didn't answer right away, but at least she took her hand out of the box for a moment. Then she drew in a deep breath. "Well, I am looking for it," she admitted. "I started to think on my way over here. You know, you did talk a lot about wanting a diamond ring. And now one is missing. I was wondering if this really was such a coincidence, after all."

"How *could* you?" I cried. "I thought you were my best friend." I felt as if I might start to cry any minute, but I fought back my tears.

"I just figured that before this went any further, I better make sure you really didn't have the ring," said Claudia.

"And?" I asked. "*Are* you sure, now that you've gone through all my private belongings?" I felt less like crying then. I was starting to get mad.

"I'm sure. "At least, I'm *pretty* sure."

That did it. "I can't believe you don't trust me," I said. "Anyway, if I did take the stupid ring, do you think I'd keep it in my jewelry box, where any fool could find it?"

Claudia just stared at me.

Oh, great, I thought. That was brilliant. Now I sounded as if I *had* taken the ring. "Look, search my whole room if you want," I said. "I don't care."

"I don't want to search your room," said Claud. "In fact, I don't even want to *be* in your room anymore."

"Well, that's good," I said. "Because I'm kicking you out."

"Don't bother kicking me out," she said. "I'm leaving." She left without another look at me, slamming the door behind her. I opened it right away. I heard her run downstairs to the phone in the kitchen. I heard her call her father and ask him to pick her up. And then I heard her say something to my mother, and march through the front door to wait outside.

Some best friend, huh?

I *hate* it when Claud and I fight. I really do. We don't fight that often, but every time we do, it's just awful. The world can be a very lonely place when you and your best friend aren't speaking to each other.

All day Sunday, I thought of calling Claudia. I wanted to make up with her. But you know what? As much as I wanted to make up, I did *not* want to apologize. I figured she was the one who owed me an apology. After all, best friends are supposed to trust each other, right?

So I sat around and waited for her to come to her senses and call *me*. "Stacey?" she'd say. "I'm really sorry. I don't know what came over me. Of course you didn't steal that ring. Can you ever forgive me for doubting you?"

But the phone never rang. Well, that's not entirely true. It rang three times. Once someone from the subscription department of the local newspaper called, wanting to know if we would like to subscribe. Another call was from my dad. He wanted to find out when I was planning to visit him next. And the third call was a wrong number.

In between calls, I spent the weekend hanging out in my room: doing homework, reading magazines, listening to my Walkman, and thinking. After a weekend like that, it was almost a relief to go back to school on Monday.

Claudia avoided me in the halls that day. I know she saw me, because I saw her. But we didn't make eye contact, and we didn't say hello. I skipped lunch in the cafeteria and went to the library instead. I sat at one of the corner tables and ate my sandwich and apple quietly, so the librarian wouldn't kick me out for eating in there.

I was feeling pretty lonely.

But I was also feeling kind of good. I had decided that something had to be done about the situation with the Gardellas, and I thought I might have come up with a solution to the problem. It wasn't a perfect solution, but it was something. I would tell everybody about it at the club meeting this afternoon. If they liked my idea, I'd go ahead with it.

I was careful not to get to the meeting too

early that day; I did *not* want to be alone with Claudia. When I *did* get there, I felt funny walking up the stairs to her room. I've walked up those stairs so many times, and just about every other time I've been looking forward to seeing my best friend. But that day I was dreading it.

I was relieved when I walked into club headquarters and saw Kristy, Dawn, and Jessi already there. They looked up and said hello when I walked in, but Claud ignored my entrance.

She was sitting on the bed next to Dawn, so no way was I going to sit on the bed, too. I didn't really want to sit in my other usual spot — the desk chair — because then I'd be facing Claud. I decided to sit on the floor near Jessi, with my back against the bed. That way I wouldn't have to look at Claudia *or* be near her.

I don't know if everybody was talking before I arrived, but they sure weren't saying anything once I sat down. The room was very quiet. I could hear the cellophane rustling as Claudia unwrapped a pack of Twinkies. (Of course, I wasn't looking at her, so I wasn't *positive* they were Twinkies; they might have been Devil Dogs or Funny Bones. But my guess is that they were Twinkies, because those are favorites of Claud's.)

After a couple of minutes I heard footsteps on the stairs and then Mary Anne and Mallory came into the room. Mary Anne gave me a funny look when she saw where I was sitting, but then she shrugged and took a seat on the bed. Mal sat on the floor next to Jessi, and smiled at me.

"Okay," said Kristy. "We're all here and it's five-thirty. Let's get started." She leaned back in the director's chair and straightened her visor. "Does anybody have any club business?"

Somehow I wasn't ready yet to tell them my idea. But there was something else I had to do. "Well, it's Monday," I said. "Dues day."

Everybody groaned.

"You know," said Claudia. "I don't think we should have to *pay* dues when we're not earning any money."

"But we always pay dues!" said Mary Anne. She sounded shocked.

"That's right," agreed Kristy. "We need that money in our treasury, no matter how slow business is."

"It was just a thought," said Claudia crossly.

Now I *really* didn't want to look at her. I pulled out the manila envelope that we use for a treasury and held it in back of me, waiting for someone on the bed to take it from me so I wouldn't have to turn around.

"Okay," said Kristy, once the envelope had made its rounds. "Now listen. We've all heard about what happened with the Prezziosos on Saturday, right?"

Oh, great. If Claud had told everybody *that* story, then she must have also told them about our fight. Did they feel the same way she did? Did they suspect me, too? It didn't seem like it. At least the others were speaking to me and acting more or less like my friends. So even if Claud had told them, maybe they hadn't made up their minds who to side with.

"Yeah," said Jessi, answering Kristy's question. "And I can't believe the nerve of those Gardellas."

"What they're doing isn't right," said Mallory.

"It's not," agreed Mary Anne. "But they *are* doing it. And we've got to figure out how to deal with it."

"Right. Before our reputation is completely trashed," said Dawn. "This club could go out of business if we don't do something."

"But what can we do?" asked Claud. "I mean, they're adults, and we're just kids. We can't go around telling everybody that the Gardellas are liars."

"No," said Kristy. "But they're not exactly liars, anyway. They really think Stacey took that ring."

"And they think our clients have a right to know," said Mal. "What a mess."

"Well," I said, realizing that it was now or never. I cleared my throat. "I have an idea," I paused.

"Well, go on!" said Kristy. "We need all the ideas we can get."

"I was thinking," I said. "I know something has to be done, and I figure I'm the one to do it. I hope my plan will save the club — and maybe it will also help me prove I'm not an awful person and a thief."

"We know you're not, Stacey," said Mary Anne.

"Well, most of us do, anyway," I said. "I know I shouldn't feel like I have to prove myself to my *friends*. . . . " I could feel Claudia looking at the back of my head. I hoped she felt bad about what she had done.

"So what's your plan?" asked Kristy.

I took a deep breath. "I thought I would

offer to baby-sit for free for the Gardellas, until the price of the ring is paid off."

Everybody was quiet for a moment. Then Jessi spoke up. "Wow," she said, quietly. "But you didn't take the ring."

"I know," I said. "And I know I shouldn't have to pay them back for it. I don't even know what they'll think when I tell them my plan. Will they think I'm proving I'm innocent — or just admitting I'm guilty?"

"Whatever they think, *I* think it's a good plan," said Kristy. "It'll clean up your record with them, and then the club can start fresh. Anyway, it's the best idea we've heard yet. I think you should go for it."

Everybody else seemed to agree, too, so I decided to call Mrs. Gardella up right away. I dialed her number and when she answered I told her who it was. She sounded a little surprised.

"Why, Stacey," she said. "I didn't expect to hear from you."

"I know," I said. "But I was hoping I could clear things up between us." Mrs. Gardella didn't say anything, so I plunged ahead. "I was wondering if you would let me baby-sit for free for you until I've paid off whatever the ring cost."

She was quiet for a moment, which made me nervous. Then she said, "Well, that's very generous of you, considering that you insist that you didn't take the ring."

"I didn't," I said. "But somehow I feel responsible for the fact that it's missing. Anyway, maybe if you let me have another chance to sit for you you'll learn to trust me again."

There was another long pause on the other end of the line. I raised my eyebrows at Kristy while I waited for Mrs. Gardella to make up her mind. Finally, she said, "I guess it's only fair to give you a chance to make things right. But I'm afraid I just don't feel comfortable leaving you alone in the house. I'll agree to your offer, but only if someone else from your club comes with you, at least the first time."

"Uh, well, okay. How about the club president, Kristy Thomas?" I asked, raising my eyebrows at Kristy again.

"That would be fine," said Mrs. Gardella. "Would you like to start this Friday?"

"Sure," I said. "Let me check with Kristy." I put my hand over the mouthpiece of the phone and whispered to Kristy. "She says it's okay but she doesn't want me to come alone. Would you come with me? This Friday?"

Kristy nodded. "Seems kind of weird to me," she said. "But if it will save the club, sure, I'll do it."

I took my hand off the mouthpiece. "That's fine," I said to Mrs. Gardella. "What time would you like us to be there?"

She asked us to come at eight-thirty. She still sounded a little hesitant, but I guess she realized how badly I wanted the chance to prove myself.

I hung up once we'd agreed on the details, and gave a big sigh. "Wow," I said. "This is really getting complicated."

"Yeah," said Mallory. "And do you realize that we *still* don't know what really did happen to the ring?"

I smiled at her. I was glad she trusted me.

"Do you think it really could have been taken by the burglar?" asked Jessi, her eyes round. So she believed me, too. Not *everybody* was a traitor, like my supposed best friend.

We spent the rest of the meeting trying to figure out what could have happened to the ring. Mary Anne wondered if the baby might have swallowed it. Dawn thought Mrs. Gardella might have dropped it down the drain without noticing. Jessi seemed convinced that it was the burglar. And Kristy figured that it had just been misplaced and the Gardellas hadn't looked very hard for it.

The only person who didn't offer a theory was Claud. But I knew what *she* thought, and I was just as glad she didn't speak up.

The meeting passed quickly — so fast, in fact, that I was surprised when I heard Kristy say, "Okay, that's it for today!"

The phone hadn't rung once. We all realized it at the same moment.

"Oh well," said Dawn. "There *is* a bright side to all of this. At least if we're not going on jobs, we don't have to write in the club notebook!"

Kristy threw a pillow at her, but the rest of us cracked up. It was nice to know we could still find something to laugh at.

On Friday, Kristy came to my house for supper after our club meeting. Then my mom drove us to the Gardellas'. I felt a little down, because (if my plan worked) I'd be sitting for free for a long, long time. Even so, I was determined to do my best, because it was the only solution I could see to my — and the club's — problem.

As we stood on the Gardellas' front porch, ringing the bell, I looked over at Kristy. I was suddenly really, really happy that she was there with me. "Thanks," I said, hoping she'd know what I meant.

"No problem," she answered. "I just hope I don't have to come with you *every* time!" We laughed.

Mrs. Gardella answered the door, and I was relieved to see that she was acting normal. Normal for Mrs. Gardella, that is. After I'd introduced Kristy to her, she gave us the same house tour that she'd given me the first time I'd been there. She kept going on about how Bird had had an upset stomach lately, and explaining that we were to feed him only a little bit of food at a time. Mouse was feeling fine, but he hadn't had much attention that day, so she wanted us to be sure to play with him once Tara was asleep.

"And Tara here," she said, boosting the baby up to her shoulder, "will need a bottle soon, and then she'll be ready for bed."

We nodded.

"I hope this works out for us, Stacey," Mrs. Gardella said, looking at me. "Even when our nanny comes back, it would be nice to have a back-up sitter. We'd like to be able to trust you to be that person."

At first I didn't know what to say. "I hope so, too," I said finally.

As soon as the door closed behind Mr. and Mrs. Gardella, Kristy looked at me in amazement. "Can you believe them?" she asked. "They treat their animals as if they were people!"

"I know. They're something else. But isn't Tara cute?"

Kristy leaned toward Tara, who was sitting on the couch between us. "You *are* cute," she said, letting Tara grab onto her finger. "You are about the cutest baby I've ever seen. And you can't help it that your parents are lunatics."

"Kristy!" I said. I couldn't believe she said that.

"What?" Kristy replied. "Tara can't understand a word I'm saying. And I was only kidding, anyway. But speaking of lunatics, did you hear that report on the radio last night? The police still haven't caught the burglar."

"I know," I said. "That makes me nervous. Let's make sure all the doors are locked." I'd never thought much of Jessi's theory that the burglar was the one who took Mrs. Gardella's ring, but now the idea sent a shiver down my spine. Suppose he *had* been in the house with me that night?

Kristy checked the front door. "It's locked," she said. "And I'll put the chain on, too — just in case."

I made sure the windows were locked. Then we checked the back door and the basement door. "Do you think we should look around upstairs?" I asked. "I mean, to make sure the burglar isn't under a bed or something?"

"Oh, Stacey," said Kristy. "Don't be silly. Burglars don't hide under beds." Then she glanced at me. I must have looked scared. "Okay," she said. "If it'll make you feel better."

We trooped upstairs (I was carrying Tara) and checked inside each closet and under every bed, including Tara's crib. Ordinarily, neither of us would ever go around looking in our clients' closets. We *never* snoop. But these were not normal circumstances. Mouse and Bird followed us from room to room, sniffing each place as if they were also checking for burglars.

"Okay?" Kristy asked. "I think we're the only people in the house, don't you?"

"Yup," I said. "Nobody here but us chickens." That's from an old joke my dad taught me when I was little — about a thief in a hen coop who says that line when the farmer yells, "Who's in there?"

Kristy laughed. I guess she'd heard the joke from Watson. Then she said, "Can I give Tara her bottle? I haven't taken care of a baby in a while, and I miss it."

"Sure," I answered. We headed for the kitchen and warmed up the bottle. When it was ready, Kristy sat on the couch with Tara, feeding her. I watched quietly. Tara's eyelids were drooping, and I knew that if we didn't startle her she'd fall asleep easily.

Sure enough, by the time the bottle was half empty, Tara was practically asleep. Kristy lifted her to her shoulder and burped her, then carried her carefully upstairs. I followed — and Mouse and Bird followed *me*. The minute Tara was in her crib, she started to breathe deeply.

"Out like a light," said Kristy. "What an easy baby to sit for!"

"*She's* easy," I said. "But these guys are another story." I pointed at Mouse and Bird, who were looking at us hopefully. "I guess they know it's their dinnertime," I said.

Kristy turned out the light in Tara's room and we went downstairs. Preparing dinner for the animals took longer than getting Tara's bottle warmed, but finally everything was ready. I put out just a little bit for Bird, but he ate it right up so I gave him seconds. Mouse scarfed down *his* dinner before I could even turn around.

After the animals had eaten, we all went into the living room. Bird curled up underneath the coffee table (one of his favorite spots, according to Mrs. Gardella), but Mouse seemed to want to play. He batted at our ankles when we tried to talk, demanding attention. There were some cat toys in a small basket next to the couch, and I pulled one out.

"A mouse for a Mouse," I said, throwing it down near him. He jumped on the little stuffed mouse immediately, grabbing it in his mouth and shaking it back and forth.

"What's he *doing*?" I asked.

"Um, he's killing it," said Kristy. "If it were a real mouse, that would break its neck. I saw Boo-Boo do it once."

"Oh, ew!" I said. "That's disgusting." Just then, Mouse took the toy in his mouth, got up, and walked out of the room. A couple of minutes later, just as Kristy and I were starting to talk about this new substitute teacher we both have, he came back in. Without the toy.

"Did you lose it?" I asked. "Well, here's another." I reached into the basket and threw him a tiny little pillow that must have been full of catnip. He went crazy! He rolled all over it, and then batted it around the room. His eyes were shining so that he looked like a little tiger. Kristy thought it was really funny, but I was worried. What if he got sick from the catnip? The Gardellas would never forgive me.

I was about to take the toy away from Mouse when he got up, took the pillow in his mouth, and walked out of the room. And then, once again, he returned without it.

We kept giving him toys: little balls with bells inside them, a miniature cat with a long tail for him to chase, and another stuffed mouse. He played with them all, but then he carried each one out of the room and came back without it.

"What does he *do* with all of them?" asked Kristy.

"I don't know," I said. "But I'm going to find out." When he came back the next time, I gave him a little stuffed bird. Sure enough, after he'd played with it for a while, he picked it up in his mouth and walked off. I got up and followed him, hoping he wouldn't notice. He didn't even look over his shoulder.

Mouse headed for a desk in the Gardellas' library. He stopped in front of it, put the bird down on the rug, and then gently batted it with his paw until it rolled under the desk.

"Aha!" I said. "So this is your hiding place." I got down on my hands and knees to see what was under there. I saw the bird, the two mice, some foil balls, the ball with the bells, and the miniature cat.

"I'll get those for you," I said to Mouse.

"We're almost out of toys, anyway. We need these back." I rummaged around in a closet until I found a yardstick. Then I bent down again and used it to sweep the toys out from under the desk.

"There you go," I said. (I couldn't believe I was talking to this cat like he was a person. It must have been the Gardellas' influence.) But Mouse was nowhere to be seen. "Mouse," I called. "Where are you?"

"He's in here," called Kristy from the living room. "He got tired of waiting for you, so he found some other toys on his own."

I came in to look. Mouse had located a stash of plastic twist-ties, the kind used to tie up plastic bags, and he seemed to be in heaven. He would toss one of them in the air, and then he'd go crazy chasing it around when it landed.

Then he started to pick *those* up and carry them away. Only this time he wasn't going to the library. This time he was headed for the TV room. I was curious, so I followed him on his next trip.

Mouse headed for the corner of the rug that was under the TV. He put down the twist-tie and batted it underneath the rug where there was a little wrinkle. "You crazy cat," I said.

"You've got hiding places all over this house, don't you?"

I walked over and lifted up the rug. Sure enough, a whole pile of twist-ties was there, plus a bunch of paper clips, plus . . . *a diamond ring*! I gasped and put my hand over my mouth. "Oh, my lord," I said to myself. Then I yelled for Kristy.

She couldn't believe it. "The ring was here all along!" she said. "This is incredible."

"What should we do?" I asked.

"Let's leave everything just as it is," she said. "That way we can show it to the Gardellas when they come home."

I have to admit that I felt pretty smug as I led Mr. and Mrs. Gardella into the TV room later that night. And when I pulled back the rug, and heard Mrs. Gardella gasp, I felt even better. Now she knew I wasn't a thief.

"Oh, Stacey," she said. "I am *so* sorry. I can't believe I didn't think to check Mouse's hiding places. You wouldn't believe how many little things we've lost this way. But this is a new hiding place. I didn't even know about it."

I explained how I'd followed Mouse around to see what he was doing.

"That was smart," said Mrs. Gardella. "I

really don't know how to apologize to you. I feel terrible. First thing in the morning I'll call the Prezziosos and tell them they were right to stand up for you."

"Oh, thanks," I said. "Um, do you think you could call everyone else, too?"

"Everybody else?" she repeated. "We didn't tell anyone else. I've been so busy, with Bird sick and all."

I was surprised. Maybe it *had* just been a coincidence that we'd received so few job calls lately.

"Well, anyway, I'm glad you have your ring back," I said.

Mr. Gardella drove me and Kristy home. And when he paid us, I noticed that he gave us about double what we should have earned. I guess he felt as bad as his wife did.

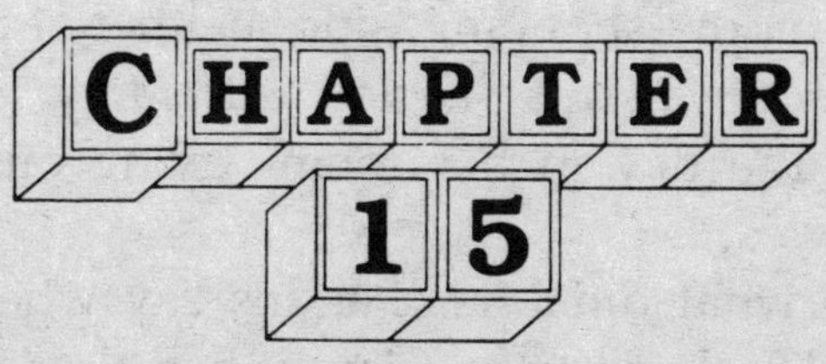

"Okay, everybody," I said. "Cough it up!" I passed around the manila envelope. It was dues day again. The Baby-sitters Club was back to business as usual.

I smiled at Claudia as she emptied out her penny jar and started to count. "Down to the last few cents, huh?" I asked. "Don't worry. You'll be rich again soon."

Claudia smiled back. "I can't believe we already have five jobs lined up for this week. Clients hardly ever call my number except during club meetings, but this week the phone has been ringing off the hook." She shook her head over the pile of pennies she'd made. "Now I've lost count," she said, starting over.

Boy, did it feel good to be friends with Claud again. We'd made up over the weekend. In fact, she had called me, planning to apologize, while I was still at the Gardellas'. So she had realized she was wrong even *before* I'd been proven innocent. That made me feel terrific. Claudia and I had spent Saturday at the mall, just window-shopping, since neither of us had any money. And Sunday was rainy, so we spent the day in her room, trying out new hairstyles.

"So what did Mrs. Perkins say when she called?" asked Kristy. Claudia had already told us about the calls she'd gotten, but we needed to hear the details.

"She said they had been on vacation, and she and her husband had really enjoyed spending time with the girls, but now they were back and she was ready to line up some sitters again," said Claudia. The Perkinses have two little girls — Gabbie and Myriah — and a baby named Laura.

"And what did Dr. Johanssen say?" asked Mary Anne.

Claudia laughed. "I already told you this," she said, "but okay. Charlotte had another strep throat and she didn't want to expose us. But Charlotte's fine now. And Stacey, you've got a job with her on Wednesday."

"Great!" I said. Charlotte's one of my favorite kids to sit for. She's almost like a little sister to me.

Claudia finished telling us about the rest of

the calls she'd received. The Newtons. The Addisons. The Braddocks. They all had very good reasons for not calling us recently, and they all needed sitters again. Our reputation was as good as ever. What a relief!

Mary Anne was going over the club record book. "Wow, are we going to be busy for the next couple of weeks," she said. "We may have to call on Shannon and Logan to help us if we get too many more jobs."

Just then the phone rang. Kristy answered it. "Oh, hello, Mrs. Gardella," she said, making a face at me. "Yes, we're glad, too. Oh, really? Well, that's nice. Thanks for letting us know. 'Bye!"

Kristy hung up. "She said she was 'so glad the mess had been cleared up,' and she was sorry — for the fortieth time." Kristy smiled at me. "She also said their nanny is back so she won't need us much anymore."

"Good!" I said. "You know what? I wasn't going to sit for them again, anyway. We don't need clients like that, when we've got all our good old regulars back."

"I agree with Stacey," said Mary Anne shyly. "I don't think we should sit for people who don't trust us and who would spread rumors about us."

Everybody nodded. "It's unanimous," said Kristy. "We won't sit for the Gardellas again, even if their nanny deserts them. We don't need business that badly."

"It's sort of sad, though," I said thoughtfully. "Tara is the sweetest baby."

"But what about Mouse and Bird?" asked Kristy. "I mean, we're *baby*-sitters, not spoiled-animal-sitters."

We all laughed. Then the phone rang again. It was Mrs. Barrett, looking for a sitter for Buddy, Suzi, and Marnie.

"They were away on a trip," said Kristy after she'd hung up. "That's why she hasn't called lately. But she says Buddy misses Mallory, and he asked for her especially. The job's on Saturday afternoon."

Mary Anne was looking at the record book. She gasped and put her hand over her mouth. "Oh!" she said. "That's right. I have a little note here saying 'Barretts to Grand Canyon.' I forgot all about their vacation." She shook her head. "Well, I'm glad they're back. And yes, Mallory is free, but so are you, Stacey," she said.

"You take the job," I said to Mal. "I've already got two others lined up."

The phone rang throughout the meeting — just like the old days. One of the last calls was from Jessi's mom, Mrs. Ramsey. She wanted to remind Jessi that she and Mr. Ramsey had tickets to the theater that Saturday, and that Aunt Cecelia would be away visiting cousins.

"I remembered," said Jessi, when the call was over. "And I'm looking forward to the job. At least I don't have to worry about that old burglar anymore."

"What?" asked Mary Anne. "Did he get caught?"

"Didn't you hear?" asked Jessi. "It was on the radio last night. I guess he wasn't the most brilliant burglar in the world. They caught him because he left his wallet at one of the houses he robbed. And get this," she went on. "The wallet was under a couch, but the family's dog pulled it out when they were sitting around watching TV!"

"I don't believe it," I said. "That's incredible! That dog must have been taking lessons from Mouse."

"And once the cops had his wallet, it wasn't too hard to find him," added Claudia. "His driver's license was in there, along with all kinds of other ID."

"Well," said Jessi. "I am so, so glad he got caught. I was scared he'd show up while I was baby-sitting somewhere."

"Do you know what to do if a burglar *does* show up?" asked Kristy. "It's important to know how to deal with a situation like that."

"Umm," said Jessi. "I guess I'd try to get the kids out of the house without attracting his attention."

"Good!" said Kristy. "That would be common sense."

"I'd never try to stop a burglar myself," added Mary Anne.

"Nobody should," said Kristy. "It's best just to try to get out of his way."

"But what about the police?" asked Mal.

"You could call them from a neighbor's house," I suggested.

"Right," said Kristy. "Get the children out of the house first, then figure out how to let the police know what's happening. The main thing is to make sure the kids are safe."

"I still hope it never happens to me," said Jessi. "I'm not sure if I could handle it without panicking."

"Of course you could," said Mal loyally. "You're not the panicky type. I'm sure you'd do fine."

"I guess," said Jessi. "I did manage to hide how scared I was that time with Becca and Squirt, so at least I know I can do that. But if I really saw a burglar — "

"Well, it'll probably never happen anyway," said Kristy. "But it's good to be prepared."

"Enough about burglars," said Dawn. "I have a proposal to make. I think we deserve a healthful pizza party, and I'm inviting you guys over this Friday. How about it?"

"Yea!" everybody cried at once.

"Anyone who has a sitting job can come late," said Dawn. "We'll make it a sleepover."

"Is there enough money in the treasury for pizza?" asked Kristy.

I checked. "There sure is," I replied. "Good thing we kept paying dues."

"Good thing," echoed Claudia, grinning at me. "By the way, Stacey, I want to give you something. I know it doesn't make up for what I did, and I know it's not exactly the jewelry you're dreaming of, but . . . "

She handed me a little box. I took it and opened it. "Oh, it's beautiful!" I said, holding up what she'd given me for everyone to see. "Did you make this?"

Claud nodded. "I'm glad you like it," she said.

I held it in my palm, looking at it. It was an earcuff (a *very* cool accessory these days) with a collection of blue stones and beads hanging from it. "I love it," I said. "Thanks, Claud." I passed the box around so everybody could take a look. "And by the way, I may get the birthstone ring after all," I said. "My mom told me last night that she and my dad talked about it, and they might go in together to get it for me for my next birthday — or for Christmas, or some other special occasion."

"All right!" cried Claud.

"Wow," said Jessi and Mallory together.

"That's great!" exclaimed Dawn.

"You're so lucky," added Mary Anne.

"Baby-sitters Club," said Kristy. She was answering the phone. It had rung one more time while we were talking. At the sound, we grinned at each other. It was good to be back in business.

About the Author

Ann M. Martin did *a lot* of baby-sitting when she was growing up in Princeton, New Jersey. Now her favorite baby-sitting charge is her cat, Mouse, who lives with her in her Manhattan apartment.

Ann Martin's Apple Paperbacks are *Bummer Summer, Inside Out, Stage Fright, Me and Katie (the Pest)*, and all the other books in the Baby-sitters Club series.

She is a former editor of books for children, and was graduated from Smith College. She likes ice cream, the beach, and *I Love Lucy*; and she hates to cook.

Look for Mystery #2

BEWARE, DAWN!

My heart skipped a beat. First the phone rang, and, according to Jenny, nobody was there when she picked it up. Next the doorbell rang, and nobody was *there*, either. What was going on?

I looked out the window again, just to be sure. There was definitely nobody there. I unlocked the door and opened it a crack, keeping the chain on. I looked all around. Then I saw something white on the front step. An envelope!

I took the chain off the door and opened it wider — just wide enough to bend down and grab the envelope. Then I stepped back inside and locked the door behind me.

I brought the envelope back to the kitchen table and sat looking at it for a minute. I had a creepy feeling about that little white packet. Finally, I opened it and pulled out the letter. Oh, man! Talk about creepy. Did you ever see those letters that kidnappers send, you know, in the movies? They're made out of all different little letters cut out of magazines and newspapers. They do that so nobody can trace their writing, I guess.

Well, that's what this letter looked like. Here's what it said:

You'd better watch out, you'd better not shout! I'm going to get you.

And it was signed, Mr. X.

I shuddered. Who could have left this awful thing on the doorstep? Was it Jenny's Mr. Nobody.

Jenny. Could she have somehow done this? I shook my head. She's only four, I reminded myself. Still, I tiptoed upstairs and checked on both girls. They were sleeping quietly, their breathing regular.

I went back downstairs and stuck the letter in the middle of my math book. "Mr. X" had definitely upset me — but I wasn't going to show the letter to any of the other club members, or tell them about this either. The Sitter of the Month had to be someone who was in control — somebody whose sitting jobs always went smoothly. I couldn't risk anyone else knowing about what had happened.

Don't miss any of the latest books in The Baby-sitters Club series by Ann M. Martin

#34 *Mary Anne and Too Many Boys*
Will a summer romance come between Mary Anne and Logan?

#35 *Stacey and the Mystery of Stoneybrook*
Stacey discovers a *haunted house* in Stoneybrook!

#36 *Jessi's Baby-sitter*
How could Jessi's parents have gotten a *baby-sitter* for her?

#37 *Dawn and the Older Boy*
Will Dawn's heart be broken by an older boy?

#38 *Kristy's Mystery Admirer*
Someone is sending Kristy *love notes*!

#39 *Poor Mallory!*
Mallory's dad has lost his job, but the Pike kids are coming to the rescue!

#40 *Claudia and the Middle School Mystery*
Can the Baby-sitters find out who the cheater is at SMS?

#41 *Mary Anne vs. Logan*
Mary Anne thought she and Logan would be together forever. . . .

#43 *Stacey's Emergency*
The Baby-sitters are so worried. Something's wrong with Stacey.

#44 *Dawn and the Big Sleepover*
A hundred kids, thirty pizzas — it's Dawn's biggest baby-sitting job ever!

#45 *Kristy and the Baby Parade*
Will the Baby-sitters' float take first prize in the Stoneybrook Baby Parade?

#46 *Mary Anne Misses Logan*
But does Logan miss *her*?

#47 *Mallory on Strike*
Mallory needs a break from baby-sitting — even if it means quitting the club.

Super Specials:
1 *Baby-sitters on Board!*
Guess who's going on a dream vacation? The Baby-sitters!

2 *Baby-sitters' Summer Vacation*
Good-bye, Stoneybrook . . . hello, Camp Mohawk!

3 *Baby-sitters' Winter Vacation*
The Baby-sitters are off for a week of winter fun!

4 *Baby-sitters' Island Adventure*
Two of the Baby-sitters are shipwrecked!

5 *California Girls!*
A winning lottery ticket sends the Baby-sitters to *California*!

6 *New York, New York!*
Bloomingdales, the Hard Rock Cafe — the BSC is going to see it all!

Mysteries:
1 *Stacey and the Missing Ring*
Stacey's being accused of taking a valuable ring. Can the Baby-sitters help clear her name?

2 *Beware, Dawn!*
Someone is playing pranks on Dawn when she's baby-sitting — and they're *not* funny.